THE CONFESSIONAL

W. J. Ferguson

Love-LovePublishing
P.O. BOX 258136 Madison, WI 53725
ISBN: 978-0-997-3200-9-1
Library of Congress Control Number: 2017936800
Title: The Confessional/ W.J. Ferguson
Digital distribution | Love-LovePublishing, 2017.
Paperback | Love-LovePublishing, 2017

DEDICATION

I'd like to dedicate this novel to my publisher, Erica Hughes, without whose hard work and inspiration would have left the idea of this novel being published as nothing more than idle conversation.

CHAPTER ONE

"Where is he?" Sebastian Roark asked the police sergeant who was closely following him into the church.

"In the confessional," The young sergeant answered.

"He's still in there?"

"Yes, sir. Nobody's touched a thing."

"You saw him? Right?"

"Yes, sir. I saw him. It was ugly. Couldn't believe my eyes. What could a priest ever have done to deserve this?"

Noticing the sergeant was so young and lacking in experience, and suspecting he might be lying to protect himself, Roark asked again with his voice a little sterner this time. "And you didn't touch a thing?"

"No, sir. I didn't touch anything."

Roark took a second or two to observe the young sergeant. He was one of those tall, good-looking blonde kids, freshly scrubbed and probably right out of the military with every intention of being a good cop and saving the world. Still much too early in his career to be thinking about pensions, family health insurance coverage, or how to deal with the kind of shit he'd have to deal with over the next forty years. Or, until he got

himself killed while on duty, whichever occurred first.

"Okay, I get that. Thank you," Then Roark
gave the young sergeant a stern look. Point-
ing to his own head, he said, "Well?"

"Sir?"

"Your hat, sergeant. We *are* in a church."

With embarrassed speed the young sergeant removed his hat. "Sorry, sir."

Roark stood for a moment, frozen outside
the entrance to the confessional. How long
had it been since he was last in a Catholic
Church? All those years, a regular attendee
and now, what's it been? Ten, fifteen years?
He'd lost track of the time.

He was a fallen-away Catholic, so being
back in a Catholic Church again for the first
time in years, it brought back memories but
memories from which he had long since
turned away. The Church was something he
was born into and, aside from his natural
mother, it was the only thing that during
his formative years, nurtured him, taught
him everything, and made him, in many
ways, what he now was. Well, almost everything. Better those memories left behind
where he last buried them.

It was an old church. Probably built
shortly after World War II when Los Angeles
became the destination of so many immi-
grants, hopeful of finding a better life.

The altar was the old traditional kind with
a life-size crucifix at the very top with a very

sad Jesus looking down onto the altar. The gold tabernacle, the place where thin wafers would later be consecrated into the very body of Jesus Christ, was the centerpiece. Ruby red carpeting covered most of the sanctuary, including two steps that led from the main level up to the altar level where the priest would say mass. The altar railing where people come every Sunday to receive the host spanned all the way across the church and separated the sanctuary from the main body where all the people would, on a typical Sunday, fill the church. On either side of the center of the sanctuary there was a smaller altar with the statue of Mary, the mother of God, on the left and on the right, some other saint he couldn't identify. Trays of red colored candle holders awaited the devout who, after making a small donation, would light a candle and pray for something or other as if lighting a candle would speed the prayer along to heaven a lot quicker. The pews in the church had a pungent familiar odor. Maybe it was the wood or maybe it was something they used to polish the pews. No mistaking that smell. He shook his head slightly as if to rid his mind of it in an attempt to turn back to business.

With a certain amount of hesitation and fear he pulled back the curtain. Inside the small chamber sat the priest, lifeless as could be, with dead eyes staring right at

Roark. He had a large, rather lethal looking knife stuck firmly into his neck. In the dim light coming from a tiny light above, Roark could see dried blood that had been running down the priest's neck, over his Roman collar, and onto his black vest.

Roark had seen a lot of dead people in his twenty years on the force but this might rank right up there with the worst, the most vicious, he had ever seen. And why? What possible reason caused this to happen? Even as hardened as he had become being a policeman for all these years, it still made him shudder just a bit and feel a rush of nausea throughout his body. He stepped back and closed the curtain.

"Who could have done such a thing as this?" Roark directed his question toward the sergeant but more rhetorically than one expecting an answer

"Probably a Protestant, is what I think."

"Shut up with that kind of talk, sergeant. Until you know the facts there's no reason to indict an entire religion."

"Sorry, sir, I'm just angry and I spoke out of anger. I'm a Catholic and this really upsets me."

Roark let the sergeant's apology go unanswered. Youth? Sometimes he got frustrated with the young bulls coming into the department. The sergeant was tall and muscular, very athletic looking. Not a wrinkle on his face. Roark winced as a feeling of jealousy swept over him. In a New York second, he admitted he'd trade places with the young man. Or at least, trade bodies. His was never anything to brag about so Roark never paid it much mind. When half the force is in the gym lifting weights and talking about the latest hand to hand fighting techniques, he was perfectly happy with his skills as an investigator, solitary as they might be. Years of neglect and his body had paid the price. Too late now, he thought.

It wasn't until then he noticed a solitary figure sitting in a nearby pew - an older man. He was wearing black pants and a white T-shirt with blue lettering that said: Los Angeles Dodgers. His upper torso was bowed slightly forward and he seemed to be staring into space, like he was in shock.

Roark looked back at the sergeant and rolled his eyes and nodded his head as if to ask for an explanation for the older man's presence.

The sergeant answered, "He called it in. He's the pastor here, he told me. He greeted me at the door when I got here. He's just been sitting there ever since."

"Good thing I asked," said Roark. "For a minute there I thought he might be the perp."

The sergeant frowned.

Roark approached the older man, probably in his sixties. Gently, he put his hand on the man's shoulder. "I understand you're the pastor."

After a moment's hesitation, the older man reacted, just now recognizing Roark's presence. "Yes," he said, in a low, toneless voice. "I'm the pastor." He looked down at his Dodger baseball shirt. "Sorry for my attire. I was at the rectory and I came over to see what happened. And, I'm not sure but I think I'm still in shock."

"Are you able to answer some questions?"

The older priest looked up. "Yes, I can do that. Whatever I can do to help."

Roark said to the sergeant, "You need to call the coroner and the crime scene guys."

Then he returned his attention to the old priest. "You are the one who found him like this?"

The old priest whispered his answer, "Yes, I did."

"I'm going to need to ask you for a few more details, Father. Are you up to answering my questions a little more clearly? Can we go outside maybe, where we can talk? Not good here, in church, I don't think."

The old priest climbed to his feet. "Perhaps we could go to the rectory. It's private there, and we can talk."

"Let me know, sergeant, the minute the crime lab or coroner gets here," Roark said to the sergeant as he guided the priest out of the back of the church.

CHAPTER TWO

Inside the rectory, the old priest, sitting behind his desk, seemed to regain his composure and became more in focus. "Do you mind, lieutenant, if I have a glass of wine to settle my nerves?" As he asked the question he had already reached into a cabinet and was pulling out a bottle of red wine and a drinking glass. Pouring a generous helping, he tasted it, looking over the brim of the glass at Roark sitting opposite him and looking puzzled. "I'm iron deficient and the doctor has told me a glass of wine will help. Plus, you must understand, how devastating this is."

Roark nodded his consent, for what it was worth. The priest held the bottle and moved it towards Roark as if to ask if he wanted any.

"I'm on duty. Any other time, Father, and I'd join you. I'm not too happy about this situation and just as upset about it as you are and a glass of wine sure might help but right now, I have to pass. Now, tell me, from the start, what exactly happened, what did you do and what did you see? And please don't leave anything out."

Now relieved that he had proven his case for having a glass of wine, the old priest took a generous swallow allowing it to roll around in his mouth and descend down to his nervous stomach. "Ah," he mouthed. "What is it you'd like to know?"

"Confession? When did it start?"

"Same as always. Every Saturday."

"Huh?" Roark grunted.

"Four to six," The priest responded.

"The deceased, he was the only one hearing confessions?"

"Inspector, can we refer to him as Father Tim? That was his name. We always go by our first, given name. It gives us an aura of approachability and humility. Don't you think?"

"Father Tim then," Roark answered with a measure of impatience. "Was he the only one hearing confessions?"

"As you can see, inspector, I'm getting up there in age," He drank a generous swallow of wine and added, "I don't hear so good any more. Would not be good when you're hearing confessions, now would it?"

"Okay, Father Tim goes to the confessional at four o'clock. Then what?"

"We have a regular schedule here, inspector. The cook arrives around 5:30 and she expects to serve dinner right after six o'clock. I'm afraid we're victims of her schedule. I hate to upset her," He then lowered his voice. "She can be a little mean when things don't go her way."

Roark was becoming a little agitated with the old priest's answers. To him they seemed evasive and evasiveness was one of the things to him, as an investigator, raised a red flag, a certain factor that he needed to make note of and reexamine. "So, six o'clock is dinner. What did I miss here, Father? If you could be a little more precise?"

Feeling like a reprimanded school boy who had misbehaved, the older priest swallowed the rest of the wine and poured another glass. "As I said, inspector, dinner is at six o'clock right after the end of confession. When Father Tim didn't return to the rectory I was alarmed. It's not a major trip, as you know. Just across the parking lot."

"So, you went looking for him?"

"Of course, what else would I have done?"

Roark took a deep breath and swallowed, studying the face of the old priest. Like the sergeant, he had close-cropped hair, totally gray. Possibly, like the sergeant, he had that look about him that indicated he might have also been an ex-Marine. His face was strong but terribly wrinkled with deep crevices. Possibly, thought Roark, from too much sun. Or, maybe too much red wine. He wasn't sure which. One thing he was sure of and that was the fact this old priest was clever and knew how to be evasive. And, just as a guess on Roark's part, he speculated that he may have been a boxer at one time. Roark could see that his arms might have been muscular until the ravages of age made the muscles shrink and the skin sag where the triceps had once been firm.

"You went looking for him? And what time, precisely, would that have been?"

"I told you, inspector. Right after six o'clock. All right. You want precise. It was probably 6:10 to be exact."

"That's when you found Father Tim, at 6:15 or so?"

"Yes. Then I called 911 and the rest you know about."

"When you found him, did you touch anything?"

"Inspector, give me some credit. I may be old but I'm not stupid. I watch a few of my favorite cop shows; so, I know the ropes."

"I'll take that as a no that you didn't touch anything."

The old priest noted the sarcasm but nodded with a shrug of his shoulders followed by another generous sip of wine.

"All right then. You found him at, roughly, 6:15 and then you went back to the rectory to call 911? Is that correct?"

"That's exactly correct, inspector."

"Then, after you made the call, you went back to the church to receive the officer who first responded?"

"Yes. I thought the police would be able to find the church a lot easier than here in the rectory."

"Roughly, how long did you wait in the church for the sergeant?"

"Ten minutes, maybe. I opened the door to the back the church. I stood out on the steps waiting."

"You didn't go back inside the church?"

"No, I didn't want to be near the scene."

"Sergeant Brady showed up and you then showed him the confessional?"

"Yes."

"And all this time you touched nothing and saw no one enter the church or leave the church other than Sergeant Brady?"

"Is that the young officer's name, Brady?"

"Father?" Roark scolded.

"I just wanted to be sure. No, inspector, I did not touch anything and I did not see anybody come into or out of the church at any time."

"All right," said Roark. "That's all for now. I may have more questions but, right now, I'm going back over to the church and wait for the coroner and crime scene guys. I'd appreciate it if you'd stay available and not talk to anyone about any of this." With that much having been said for now, he rose to leave.

The older priest mumbled, "Is there a reason for all these questions?"

"Of course. You said you watch cop shows on TV. Well, then you know. We have to know everybody's whereabouts, what they saw or didn't see. Does that answer your question?"

The old priest smiled for the first time since they first met. "Then I'm not a suspect, inspector?"

"I think you know the answer to that, Father. Everybody's a suspect until we can eliminate them. Unfortunately for you, at the moment, I can't think of a single way in which I can eliminate you from being a suspect or, shall we say, a person of interest."

"I'm a Catholic priest, inspector. In our faith we consider murder to be a mortal sin, the payment for which is to burn in hell for all eternity. You can't possibly think that I would..."

Roark cut him off with surprisingly spontaneous anger. "Father, don't go there. Being a priest does not prove you did or didn't do anything. My view of the world we live in is that there are any number of nuts out there who do some strange things because God told them to do it. So, please, don't insult my intelligence with the 'I'm a priest routine'," As he headed out, the old priest steamed. Then Roark stopped, "One more question." Then he sat back down again, staring at the old priest who folded his arms in defiance.

"Father Tim is in the confessional box for two hours. People are coming in and out of the church to give their confessions. Then they say ten 'Hail Mary's' as their penance and they leave," Then he stopped, puzzled how to phrase the rest of his question and avoid more ambiguity from the old priest.

This gave the old priest the opportunity to speak up, "Yes, that's generally how it works except sometimes the penitent is asked to say ten 'Our Father's'. What's your question, inspector?"

"During all this time, two hours, people coming and going, how is it that one man did what he did and nobody saw him do it?"

"You're asking me?" The old priest asked emphasizing the word '*me*'.

"You said you watch cop shows. I thought you might have an idea."

The old priest rubbed his chin, scratching his whiskers so much they made a noise. "It used to be, inspector, back in the days when I was a young priest that confession was a weekly affair for practically all parishioners. They came to confession on Saturday night and Mass on Sunday morning. Now? Well, things have changed. And I have to disagree with the church on this. I don't think they've changed for the better. I see a lot of changes that have hurt the church. People don't go to Mass every Sunday any more. They rarely go to confession. It's only required, technically, that you only go once a year, at Easter time. It's a shame, if you ask me, to see how far things have fallen. So, inspector, sadly, I have to tell you there's no longer a steady stream of people coming in to confession."

"How many would you say, in the course of those two hours?"

"Oh, gosh," He looked up at the ceiling as if the answer might be printed there. "Like I said, I don't hear confessions much anymore because of my hearing."

"Guess," Roark interrupted impatiently.

"Ten, twenty. Something like that."

"Okay, let's say it's only ten. Ten people in the course of two hours. That's one person every twelve minutes, if I'm not mistaken. That gives our guy who did this only about twelve minutes to come into the church, look around, commit the crime, and then make sure nobody saw him. Then leave. That's possible but highly unpredictable. If I understand the picture you're painting, there's no way anybody would know that he has twelve minutes of time to complete the job and get it done without anybody seeing him escape undetected."

"I honestly don't know, inspector. Yes, I watch TV crime shows but just for a diversion not to become a crime stopper."

"Hmmnnnnn," Roark mumbled. "I'm just talking it out with you. You understand? I thought maybe you'd have an idea I'm not seeing at the moment. That leaves me with one and only one conclusion. The only person who most likely could have pulled this off without being seen might be you. And with that thought, I'll leave you. Oh, but one more thing, if you don't mind. Can I get the name and phone number of your cook?"

The old priest turned a shade of red while nervously scribbling the requested info on a piece of paper. With head down, he pushed it across his desk, leaving it for Roark to pick up and leave.

The sergeant was waiting when Roark returned to the church. "No coroner yet," Then he asked. "How did it go with the old priest?"

"Brady, I think you can go now. I'll stay here and wait for the coroner. How did it go? I think he's hiding something and I intend to find out exactly what that is."

Driving home, after he'd met and talked with the crime scene people, all Roark could think of was how the news would hit Los Angeles the next morning. Sleepy little church on the west side of the city, half-way to Santa Monica, things shouldn't happen there that make the news. Murders happen all the time in this big city but a priest, in a little church? That will surely shake up an awful lot of people, thought Roark.

The Manson murders of Sharon Tate, the actress, and some other innocent people were a little over ten years ago now, as he recalled. My how time flies. That really shook up the city, and the nation. The murder of one priest in a little church will hardly compare to that but, still, it'll more than likely shake the city. Maybe the murder of the eighties and, to think, he's an integral part of it.

CHAPTER THREE

Sebastian Roark discovered two undeniable truths about himself when he was a teenager. One, he was never going to be a great athlete, not even a halfway decent athlete. He was average in height, strength and agility and that might be stretching it a bit. He had a great love for sports but not enough ability to be a player so why bother? Time and time again, he tried and continuously failed at sports. And failure at sports, or at anything, was a bitter pill he wasn't prepared to swallow on a regular basis.

The second truth he learned about himself was the fact he was not particularly attractive to the opposite sex. He didn't consider himself to be particularly handsome. How else did he know that? Easy. They never seemed to pay much attention to him all during high school. Whenever he decided to make a move on a particular girl that interested him the results were poor. More often than not any overtures he made were quickly turned down. It wasn't very flattering. Downright hurtful, to be honest. There were always excuses: already going out with somebody else, too busy right now, my parents are very strict with my dating, etc. etc. A few times he even got laughed at. Try that a few times and you begin to get discouraged, he told himself. So, he became a bit of a loner. Why girls anyway, he asked himself, as a now wise teenager? Why bother? Skin, bones, hair? They smelled nice, to be sure, but why bother?

After high school, he joined the Navy only to wind up for two long years riding around on ships. It was better than getting drafted into the Army but it didn't turn out the way he expected it would. And he had absolutely nothing in common with his fellow shipmates. All they wanted to do and talk about was drinking and screwing, drinking and screwing.

Quite by accident he became fascinated with guns. Whenever there was a detail that required a group to go ashore well-armed with guns he had been assigned to such detail. He loved it. Throughout his childhood, who were his heroes? Gun-toting cowboys, that's who. And what games did he play with all his friends? Shoot 'em up games. That's what they played. So, guns were his old friends.

Just the feel of the gun in his hands gave him a sense of power. It was a powerful tool and he was the master of this powerful tool. And what power it was. Pulling that sensitive little trigger. Watching it strike a hundred or more yards away, seeing that little puff of smoke or a wooden target being fractured into pieces of scrap; that was a real trip, not induced by drugs.

Towards the end of his sea duty, he applied for land duty, specifically as a shore patrolman, which was the Navy's term for a policeman. Much to his delight, his request was granted.

All decked out in his dress blues or summer whites he got to carry a gun belt and a revolver around his waist. It made him feel very special. No longer was he just an ordinary sailor. He was now a member of the Shore Patrol. Often, he wondered how he would feel, if it became necessary, to shoot someone in the line of duty. As things turned out for young Roark, he never did find out but he always felt he could, if called upon to do so.

When he got out of the Navy, the most natural and logical move for him was to join the police force. Where else could he get paid for handling guns and making sure people obeyed his legitimate commands? What better way to make a living was there than bossing people around and carrying a gun, as his enforcer?

Now it was time to come to grips with his social life. Problem was most people worked and played during daytime and early evening hours and slept at night. His hours were just the reverse. Work all night and sleep most of the day.

It wasn't long before he decided to bed a young woman, a willing participant. One nasty problem sprung up, much to his surprise, and her dismay. He couldn't get an erection. He lied to her, "This has never happened to me before. I can't understand it."

She ignored his comment, "I thought all cops were studs?"

"That's why you went to bed with me?"

She looked at the holstered gun hanging on the chair nearby. He caught the look.

Feeling guilty, he went to confession first chance he got. He went through the motion of confessing his sin. But somehow, just didn't feel it anymore.

He began to wonder. How many times could a person commit a mortal sin and be forgiven? Could he just keep on having unmarried sex the rest of his life and then confess it right up to a point just before he died and then go straight to Heaven? That was the question that bounced around in his mind as he searched for an answer. And it had to be an answer that made sense to him.

It didn't take long for him to come to a conclusion. Confession was fake. The Church was a fake. The whole thing was a fake. He stopped believing in just about everything he had previously believed in all his life.

CHAPTER FOUR

About the same time he had given up the Church and had put thought of a social life on hold temporarily, he'd been promoted to detective. No more blue uniforms. Just his regular clothes and his gun neatly holstered inside the jacket he invariable wore, hot or cold weather. Solving crimes became his new passion. It had real issues he could deal with. No more unproven theories about eternal life or sin or what happens when you die. His conclusion: nobody knows. Finding who committed whatever crime he was assigned to become his creed and his new religion. It became for him a battle of wits between he and the person who committed whatever crime Roark had been sent to solve. Maybe he'd never be a great sports hero or the second coming of Rudolph Valentino but, by God, there wasn't going to be a crime he couldn't solve, if he could help it.

That Saturday night, following the murder of the priest, he laid in bed wide awake, tossing around in his mind various alternative theories about the crime. Did the old pastor do his younger assistant in for some reason? Maybe the old dude did something wrong and the younger priest was about to report him. People have done stranger things. If not the old priest, then who? Somebody who had a grudge against that particular priest? What could the priest have possibly done to deserve such a vicious murder? Or maybe the perp just had a grudge against the Church and decided to take it out on the first priest he found available. Then his thoughts turned to what was he was going to do to find out the truth. Talk more to the pastor? Try to find out for sure who was in the church during that two-hour period? Yes, all those things, more than likely. And more: much more.

CHAPTER FIVE

Sunday morning, he went to mass in the church where the murder occurred. He felt really funny about being there but he wanted to hear the announcement that he and Father Gregory agreed needed to be made. Early on a Sunday morning, not everybody would have seen the news on TV or in the paper. He doubted there would have been any mention of it on either of those mediums. How would they have gotten the story? He left the old pastor around 7:30PM, spent time with the coroner and the crime scene people until 8:30. He imagined the coroner probably gave the details to the news media, as was his responsibility, but that might have been too late to get into print or on a TV news show. So, he asked the pastor to announce the tragedy that occurred but more importantly, ask the flock if anyone saw anything on Saturday evening to please come forward and report whatever they might have seen. Contact the police, and ask for Inspector Roark, to be exact.

Sitting in the pew, towards the back, he looked at every single guy that came into the church. Why a single guy and why look intently at anybody? Criminals often, in a crime like this, revisit the scene of the crime and revel in what they have accomplished. A young single guy? Who else would have done this? He dismissed anybody who was older than fifty or had a wife and kids. Certainly possible that somebody like that could be guilty, but not very likely. More likely, thought Roark, it would be a single guy less than fifty. Besides, he couldn't focus on everybody. He had to narrow his search somehow. Better that he trim it down. Actually, there weren't that many single guys in the church that morning. A lot of those that fit the bill were grubby teenagers probably forced to go to Mass by their parents, wearing Levis and sweatshirts. Where did respect for church go these days, Roark asked himself.

Following the announcement there was the normal result, multiple, quiet conversations rolling around the church from the front to the very back. Some of them openly wept. From what he could discern from his conversation the night before, many of them loved Father Tim. They were stunned that a priest could be murdered in church and maybe just a little puzzled why it had to be Father Tim and not the old pastor who, in the eyes of some, may have been more deserving. He was imagining all this of course but that's how his mind worked.

Unfortunately, the old pastor forgot to mention that whoever might have seen something on the previous night during confessions should report what he or she saw to the police. Either that or he intentionally decided to leave that part out. Either way, Roark was incensed but there was nothing he could do. Stop mass, stand up and make an announcement on his own? What kind of circus would that have been? And not very professional. No way could he do that. So, he just sat there and burned. And counted minutes and opportunities lost.

Sunday was wasted. He wasn't ready to go back to talk to the pastor. He couldn't even get the coroner's report or the crime scene stuff. After all, it was Sunday. After a second semi-sleepless night tossing various ideas around in his head he went into the office.

CHAPTER SIX

Monday morning couldn't come soon enough. He got to work early. A meeting was had whereby it was announced that the precinct had a murder case on its hands and Detective Roark would be assigned to the investigation.

"Hey, Sea Bass, you got that case you're working on solved yet?"

Roark's partner in the office, was Roy Culpepper. The term "partner" should be used loosely. They shared a space with two desks joined together and, because of the proximity, they knew every minute detail of what the other person was doing, at least all the details that each one of them gleaned from listening to the other guy's phone conversations. He didn't dislike Culpepper; he just thought he was a horse's ass although a somewhat useful horse's ass from time to time. The only thing he hated about Culpepper was the fact that he insisted on bastardizing Sebastian's real name calling him, Sea Bass. Culpepper fashioned himself as a comedian and this was just one of his miserable attempts at being funny.

Roark thought the bastardization of his name was stupid but he never objected or even let on that it bothered him. He simply didn't want Culpepper to know that.

The bottom line was this. Culpepper was no Rhode's scholar.

"It's in the toilet right now. Thanks for asking. Besides, it's only been a day and half and I'm fresh out of miracles."

Roark paused to give some thought whether he wanted to even waste time talking to Culpepper when he had other things he needed to do. In a moment of weakness, he decided to vent.

"Here's what I got. This priest gets wasted in a confessional in church. His pastor I don't trust. Apparently, nobody witnessed the crime. I doubt there are any usable fingerprints on the knife that killed him. I'm guessing whoever did it used gloves and wiped it down beforehand. I'll probably find out no store sells the kind of knife I saw. It looked like an old army knife, probably not manufactured any more. I've got nothing."

"That is bad. But what about this pastor? You said you don't trust him. He's what, a priest? I thought those guys were all sworn to lead perfect lives."

"He lied to me. He made it sound like he had fifteen minutes or so during which to go from the rectory where he lives to the church and back before he called the police. I called his cook yesterday and it looks like he had close to half an hour. Plenty of time to do the dirty deed and get cleaned up and make it look like he's in the clear. As you know, I don't like inconsistencies in people's statements or outright falsehoods for that matter. I think he's intentionally lying to me."

"You know what I'd do if I were you, Sea Bass. I'd go talk to the guy again. Maybe he'll crack. Maybe he wants to confess. Or maybe, just maybe, you're going at this from the wrong direction."

"And which direction might be the right one, jackass?"

"Find out more about the victim. Maybe he has a past."

"A past? What could a priest have as a past that would cause somebody to kill him and I mean really kill him? It was ugly."

"Maybe he was one of those priests, you know, that abused young boys."

"You mean a predator."

"Yeah, that one. Well? Have you thought about that?"

Roark had to pause, "You know, Culpepper, sometimes, if I listen to you long enough, out of that mouth of yours might actually come a good idea, if I live long enough."

"What are you saying, Sea Bass? You agree with me? It's not a bad idea? That would be close to the first time you've ever agreed with me, Sea Bass, on anything.

Wow, maybe I should celebrate tonight and get drunk."

As much as he hated to admit it, Culpepper, for all his considerable lack of ability, did have it right. He needed to talk to the old pastor again. He made the appointment with the usual apologies of just trying to clear up a few things. Although the old priest initially objected, Roark insisted it be that afternoon while things were still fresh on his mind. The old priest convinced Roark it would have to be the next day, assuring Roark that he was not likely to forget any single detail of what happened that night.

Chapter Seven

Roark rang the door bell at the rectory and was greeted by a lovely young woman who escorted him into the pastor's office. Once he was seated, she asked him if he wanted a cup of coffee or tea and he declined. So, she quietly shut the door and left them alone.

"Who's that, Father?" Roark asked.

"My new housekeeper. The one you questioned on Sunday informed me she would be taking a leave of absence."

"Her replacement is kind of young and cute, if you ask me. But then, that wouldn't matter to you now would it, Father? But, let me ask. Don't you ever, for a just moment, get tempted?"

"Inspector Roark, please, please tell me you didn't come here to question my virtue. Yes, she's an attractive young lady but, as you well know, or at least I think you know, as priests we are sworn to complete and utter chastity. Do I ever get tempted? Of course. I'm human. And temptation is always with us as the devil never stops his endless effort to destroy us. But chastity is so important."

"With all due respect, isn't that a little unnatural, Father?"

"Unnatural?" The old priest grabbed his chin. "What you're suggesting, Inspector, is that man is made solely for the purpose of procreating the race, at all times giving in to his visceral desires, with no ability to live beyond animal instincts regarding sex and things of that nature."

"I hadn't thought about it exactly in those terms but, yeah, I guess that's what I'm suggesting."

The priest reached into his desk and pulled out a pack of cigarettes, slowly lighting one of them. "Do you mind?" When Roark ignored the question, the old priest continued, "Yes, Inspector, I have a few vices. A few too many maybe. A glass of wine and these cigarettes. It's too early in the day for wine plus she..." He nodded towards the door where the young housekeeper had exited. "She wouldn't approve of it and I do have to set a good example. Cigarettes? All she'll say is they're not good for my health and they stink up my office."

"It seems then I'm a bad influence on you?"

"How do you mean?"

"Whenever I ask you a question you don't like you get nervous and pull out either wine or a pack of cigarettes. That should tell me something."

"Inspector, please. Allow an old priest to have a couple of vices. Nervous, inspector? Why I love your questions. They intrigue me," He took a long pull on the cigarette and blew the smoke up into the ceiling. "Do you know what it's like, Inspector, sitting here every day listening to everybody's problems? Some of these people are pathetic. Instead of a priest they need to see a psychiatrist. But I have to pretend to be sympathetic and say kind words that will make them feel better. Tell them to pray knowing full well, as I do, that prayers are never answered."

"Never answered, Father. I'm appalled. In shock, actually. I never imagined I'd hear that from a priest."

"That's never to leave this room, Inspector. A bit of candor on my part. Sorry about that. Hope I didn't offend you."

"Offend me? No. It doesn't offend me at all. But I'm intrigued. How can a man of God, if that's what you call yourself, feel that prayers are never answered?"

"I'm an educated man, Inspector, and I'm not a fool, and I believe I'm capable of separating fact from fiction. I believe there's a God and he expects a certain code of behavior. If we violate that code of behavior, then we will be held accountable. Hell? Perhaps not. That's a little strong: hell for all eternity? Not very likely. But some kind of punishment, I'm sure. So, over the years, in my youth, yes, I have counseled my flock to pray. Pray for good health, pray for riches, pray to get a good job, pray to marry the right person. You name it. Did the prayers ever get answered? Not to my knowledge. Oh, sure, there have been a few cases where something somebody prayed for came true. A cure for an illness, perhaps. But, was its prayer or just the power of modern medicine? A good job? Was it prayer or just getting your resume into the right hands at the right time?" He paused to take another pull on the cigarette then ground it out into an ashtray he pulled out of the draw of his desk.

Roark shifted in his seat, exhaling, clearly showing he was getting tired of this.

"Am I boring you, inspector?" The old priest asked with as much sincerity as he could muster.

"Not in the least. I was raised a Catholic and now I've fallen away; I guess is the correct term. So, I'm fascinated by your comments. Please do continue."

"And my comments never leave this room?"

"Whatever you might think of me, Father, I'm a man of my word. So long as it has nothing to do with this case, whatever you tell me never leaves this room."

"You know what we're trained to tell people when God doesn't answer their prayers when they want their prayers to be answered?" Roark rose in his chair, waiting. "We tell them it was God's will. A child dies. They prayed as hard as a person is capable of praying that the child will live and yet, in the end, the child dies. They come to me. What else can I tell them? They didn't pray hard enough? There is no God? No, I tell them the only thing I can tell them. It was God's will the child died. That doesn't help, of course, but it gets me off the hook." He ceremoniously lit another cigarette as if a burden had been lifted off his shoulders.

"I see your dilemma," Roark added feebly, not knowing what else to say.

"What would you do, inspector?"

Roark shrugged his shoulders, "Not my problem, Father."

The old priest forced a laugh, blowing smoke towards the ceiling. Roark had this vision that the young lady was just above them, in one of the bedrooms, and was now slowly being gassed with cigarette smoke.

"No, it's not your problem. It's definitely mine and one of these days I might figure out how to solve it," The old priest waited for some kind of response from Roark. When there was none forthcoming, he continued as if it didn't matter. "Maybe I just need to learn some new answers, some new ways to put people's minds at rest and, at the same time, keep my sanity."

Roark sat up straight in his chair a second time, "However you deal with your personal dilemma is beyond my pay grade so let's get to the reason I came here. I do have more questions for you, Father. About the case."

"Shoot, inspector. I'm getting to be an old man and I'm afraid I've taken up too much of your time talking about my problems. How can I help you?"

"Tell me about Father Tim." Roark asked.

CHAPTER EIGHT

Next morning Roark was back at his office still as perplexed as before. The old pastor was no help when it came to shedding light on Father Tim. All the old pastor kept saying was how good a priest he was, "Played by the book, I guess you'd call it. Never deviated. Never took a short cut. Me? Yeah, sometimes. I have to admit, I fudge a little-- but Father Tim? Never."

And so it went, a litany of praises for the recently deceased. After a while Roark stopped listening and the old pastor rambled on.

He next squeezed in a visit to the coroner and the crime scene people. The info they had was routine, as expected, and quite preliminary. Nothing unusual. No telltale evidence that they could find.

"Sleeping in Sea Bass? Half the morning is gone. Have you solved that murder yet?"

Roark just sat there, ignoring Culpepper much like he'd ignore a fly on his arm. He knew it was there but it didn't bother him and he didn't want to spend the time or the energy to swat it. He was deep in thought.

Then, unable to control himself he blurted out his frustration, "The coroner says just what we thought. Long sharp knife direct through the neck hitting an artery. Almost instant death. A paralyzing wound."

"That's too bad," said Culpepper trying his best to be sympathetic, an emotion that clearly didn't visit him very often.

"Crime scene guys got nothing. The only finger prints are those of the victim." Roark paused to think for a moment. I guess the poor guy was trying to pull the knife out of his neck but never made it. Outside of that, nothing."

"That's really too bad. Hey, what did the pastor say about the possibility of the victim being one of those, you know, predators?"

"He was kind of pissed at me even asking the question. He said, sure, every priest, at this point in time, as a result of all the media attention, is a suspect of being a predator. Truth be known, it's less than one per cent of all the clergy, according to him anyway," Roark thought back to the old priest's actual words. "He said, if there was any truth to that, any suspicion, he would have known about it and would have reported it."

"That's kind of lame. Reported to whom? And supposing that person does nothing. Then what?"

"Shit, I don't know. What am I supposed to do, put him on the rack and pull his fingernails out? I sort of have to go easy here."

"Yeah, I see your problem," mused Culpepper. Roark said nothing. "Anyway, good luck with the case," he added, sarcastically, to break the silence. "Hey, I almost forgot. You got a visitor. Got here half hour ago. I said you were out and I could handle things but..."

"Who is he? Did he say?"

"It's not a he. And by the looks of things I'd say you better let me handle this. She's a looker. One of those babes that's built for pleasure, if you know what I mean."

"Leave it alone, jackass. Where is she?"

Chapter Nine

He found her in the waiting room and, for once, Culpepper was right about something. She was a looker. Even sitting down, as she was, he could tell she was quite shapely. As Culpepper had said: built for pleasure. His immediate reaction was one of extreme delight but then it could be trouble too. Last thing he needed was female problems. Still, she was a beauty and that was hard to ignore. Fairly long blonde hair. Very little make-up but then she didn't need it. Full lips, the kind a man wants to kiss, with just a hint of gloss. She was nobody's kept woman that was for sure, because the dress she had on was about as plain as you can imagine. Probably bought it a JC Penny, he guessed.

He cleared his throat, "Can I help you, miss? I'm Detective Roark. You wanted to see me?"

She looked up at him and at first, seemed startled, but then her look relaxed.

"Yes. I did," She said almost like she was apologizing. Standing up, she smoothed out her dress and waited for him to make the next move.

Roark wondered why she seemed nervous but then, he reasoned, it might be her very first time in a police station and that shakes a lot of people.

"Come this way, Miss. I'll lead the way," Instead of going to his desk where he knew Culpepper would be hanging around with his tongue hanging out of his mouth, salivating, he took her to an interrogation room. Once settled in, he thought she would relax and enjoy the privacy. It didn't work. He noticed her continuously looking out the window of the office, intently watching the people in the big room milling about, busily doing their duties. "You seem to be a little nervous, Miss. Is anything wrong?"

She hesitated, then blurted out, "I don't like police stations. They scare me."

"Yeah, kind of scary isn't it with all these guys walking around with guns and so forth."

She nodded.

"Well, what can I help you with?"

"I was told you're the one investigating the murder of that priest, poor Father Tim."

"Yes. Yes, I am," he said without any show of emotion. "But, wait. Who told you this?"

"Why Father Gregory told me. Father Gregory at the rectory."

"Father Gregory told you? And why, may I ask, would you be talking to him about the death of Father Tim? And, let me make a minor correction. It's not officially a murder yet."

"Oh," was all she could say, clearly surprised by his statement. "That's what Father Gregory said it was."

"Well, Father Gregory's just reacting to the most logical explanation."

"What other explanation could there be?" Her mood had suddenly changed from being very passive and nervous to more of an aggressive attitude, like she was putting him on the spot.

Now it was time for Roark to think this through for just a moment. Until he had uttered those words, he hadn't given the slightest thought to the priest's demise being anything other than murder. His response to the young woman was purely a knee-jerk reaction that any law enforcement person would have made to someone who's not close to the investigation. Now he had to defend his statement. Even still, it made him uncomfortable having to explain alternate theories of a crime scene to a lay person, especially to a young woman who would probably not understand it anyway.

"Officially, I have to say it could possibly be suicide, I suppose."

"Oh, my god," she said releasing the purse she had been clutching, putting both hands up to her face. "How awful. I really don't think...I mean, he was such a good man, Father Tim. He would never do that."

Roark was puzzled by her last comment but let it pass, "I'm not saying he did. I'm just saying, officially, I can't rule it out. Do you understand?"

"Yes," she said, returning both hands to again clutch her purse much like a security blanket.

"I didn't get your name, miss."

"It's Kitty. Kitty Meadows. I'm sorry. I should have told you that."

"It's all right," Roark answered waiving his hand as if to remove her apology. "I should have asked. You'll have to forgive me; I'm struggling a little here with my list of questions."

"You have a list of questions?"

"Well, not actually. Not a real list. Just a list in my mind."

"Oh, I see."

"Okay, let's start from the top. Why would you be asking Father Gregory about what happened?"

"I didn't know who else to ask. He made that announcement at Mass on Sunday and I was miserable all day. I didn't know what to do. I had to talk to somebody and he was the only one I could think of to talk to."

"I see. So, you just thought it'd be helpful to talk to somebody about what happened? You chose Father Gregory. It didn't occur to you to call the police like he mentioned in church?" Knowing no such announcement

had been made, he threw it out there anyway.

"I wasn't thinking very clearly, I guess,
and you must think I'm silly, inspector. I
know I'm not explaining myself very well.
You see I saw him. He was in the church."

"Who? Who was in the church?" Roark's
voice rose an octave and he sat forward in
his chair.

"It was the man who murdered Father
Tim."

CHAPTER TEN

When the interview was over with Kitty Meadows, Roark returned to his desk and slumped down in his chair, emotionally exhausted.

"What's the matter, Sea Bass, she wear you out? I told you she was a looker. I mean, wow."

"Huh? What did you say?" Roark reacted to Culpepper's tirade, shaking his head to get out of his self-induced trance.

"I said she was a looker, didn't I? You in love, now?"

"Stifle it, jackass. I'm not in love. Especially, not with a witness anyway. There are rules against that sort of thing."

"Oh, c'mon, Sea Bass. Just a little pitter-patter of the old ticker there? Right? Wait a minute. You said a witness? Really? A witness to your murder? Wow. Some guys get all the luck. But, wait. You better let me examine her to make sure she's telling you the truth."

"Sit down, and shut up before you get a hard-on. She said she saw the guy minutes before it happened. Then she left, so she's not sure. I asked what did he look like and

she's not sure. I asked her what was he doing when she observed him in church and
she doesn't remember. I can just see it now.
When the lawyer for this guy asks her these
same questions. She won't know a thing."

"Ah, bad luck, Sea Bass. I thought for a
moment there you had a break in the case."

"Me, too. I guess not. Well, just to be sure
I asked her if she could do an artist sketch?
She didn't know what that was. It was like I
was asking her to walk barefoot on hot
coals."

"You were obviously too tough on her.
Like I said, maybe I should examine her. I
mean interview her."

"You get ten feet close to her, and I'll cut
your balls off and stuff them in your
mouth."

"Hey, hey, Sea Bass. She got to you then.
Didn't she?"

The two men stopped in their tracks and
just sat there across from each other, each
one in thought. While Culpepper was thinking how he might have positioned himself
better with the witness and how to further
antagonize Roark, Roark was just thinking,
going over each detail in his mind and coming up with blanks.

"I don't blame you, Sea Bass. Go for it. I
won't stand in your way. Even though, I
think she'd like me better."

"Culpepper, do you have anything better
to do than annoy me? We're supposed to be

on the same team. We're both fighting crime, right? Nothing you're saying is helping?"

"Okay. I get that. You're right. Okay. She saw a guy she thinks was the perp. She can't describe him and probably can't pick him out of a lineup, much less, or help a sketch artist. Am I right?"

"You got it."

"Okay, did she notice anything about his movements? Did he limp? Was he big, like a football player, or small like a jockey? Did he wear a hat?"

"Nobody wears a hat in church."

"Okay, forget the hat. Was he...possibly right-handed?"

"What difference would it make whether he was right-handed or not and how the hell would she know if he was right-handed? Roark stopped then stood up, siddenly. "Wait. Wait a minute?"

"Yeah, yeah, Sea Bass? Wait a minute? Did I say something important? Right-handed, right? That would help your case? If he was right-handed you've just reduced the perp list in half, right?"

"That would be true, jackass, if fifty percent of the world's population was right-handed; but it's not. It's more like eighty percent, I think."

"Well, okay then. Maybe he was left-handed."

Roark was still deep in thought, oblivious to anything else Culpepper might be musing. Then he said, "I fucking forgot."

"What? What did you forget?"

"What side of the neck was the wound," Then, as if talking to himself, he mumbled. "It was the left side, now that I'm thinking about it, visualizing it in my mind. The left side, I think. That would indicate a right-handed person. I saw him there but it was three days ago. Now, I'm not so sure."

"Ask the coroner," Culpepper said with a smile on his face that closely resembled that of a cat catching a mouse.

Chapter Eleven

Roark wasted no time hustling over to the coroner's office for his second visit. She was busy looking at various x-rays and showed her surprise upon seeing Roark so soon after their initial meeting. She was a studious looking lady in her early or late forties...he couldn't guess. The only thing he was sure of was that she was rather plain. Her clothes matched her persona. Save for two small earrings she made no obvious attempt at looking feminine, "You forget something, Detective?"

Wow, he thought. Somebody referred to him by the title he preferred: detective. He never liked lieutenant. Made him sound like he was an officer in the foreign legion. Never liked being called inspector either. Made him think of the bumbling character Clousseau, in the movies. One thing for sure, when it came to his job, Roark considered himself to be no bumbling fool: just the opposite. A serious detective.

"Yes, I did," he said. "I wonder if I could ask you a few more questions."

"But of course." She smiled, a smile that was more plastic than genuine.

"The wound?" Roark blurted out. "Just confirm what I think I remember. The wound, it was on the left side of his throat, right?"

She wrinkled her nose giving the question due thought. To be sure, she wanted to be precise. That was her job. "Left side," she said. "Why, what are you thinking? Right-handed perp?"

"Either that or..." he paused. "Or, maybe a self-inflicted wound?"

"I doubt that very much, Detective."

"Why is that?"

"Oh, the amount of thrust that would have been required to jam a knife in a person's own neck. Let me show you." She picked up a ball point pen from her desk. Think of this as the knife. I'm right-handed, see? So, I swing my right arm up into my neck area". She did so with considerable speed stopping just short of her neck with the tip of the pen. You see; it's just too short a trip from here to there. Not enough leverage. Agree?"

He puckered his lips, wondering, "Thanks for the demonstration. I think you're lucky, doc."

"Why's that?"

"The point on the pen was retracted. Good thing."

"You noticed."

"I try to notice everything."

"Well, did you happen to notice the deceased was sitting down, in a cramped space? It would have made it a little more difficult than me standing here with lots of space and more leverage than a person sitting would have had."

"You got me there, Doc. But you're forgetting one thing. He was a guy and maybe this might not be the politically correct thing to say but guys usually have more arm strength than you ladies."

"Sorry there, Roark. Your male chauvinism is showing. I should point out I lettered two years in college as a varsity rower. I'll bet I could even out arm wrestle you."

Roark shrugged his shoulders in submission, "Not today, but maybe someday, you'll get your chance to try."

"Careful what you wish for, Roark. You wouldn't want a woman showing you up, now would you? Anyway, I've got real work to do here. Are we done? You said you had a couple of questions."

"Yeah, I was just wondering. If the guy got the knife in his neck from an attacker, why wouldn't he have had time to put his hand up to defend himself."

"Did you happen to notice that it was dark in that little space, Roark? Hardly enough light to see anything. You know why that is, Roark?"

"Why it's dark in there?"

"Yeah. That's so the priest can't see the people coming in to confession and they can't see him."

"You're forgetting one thing, Doc. There was a little light on, remember? Enough light for me and you, when we first looked in there to see clearly what had happened."

"Good point, Detective. Very good point. This shows exactly why you're a detective who solves crime while I'm just a doctor who explores human cadavers to find out things that you already know, like how a person died. There's just one thing wrong with your analysis."

"Yeah, what's that?"

"The light has a switch, Detective. Think about it, when the perp entered the space the light was probably off. There's no way the priest would have seen who it was or what was happening. Until it was too late. My guess is the perp had a mini flashlight and when he shined in the eyes of the priest he was, for a few seconds anyway, powerless to move, not being able to see a thing with a bright light shining in his eyes. Just my guess, Detective."

"Okay, Doc. You made your point and you're probably right about the flashlight. I hadn't thought about that. Thanks. Anyway, I still have to keep an open mind. Did he do himself in or did somebody do it for him? And why."

"My bet is he had help. Just my professional opinion, as a coroner, that's all."

"Just so I know, Doc. How long would it take for a guy to die with a knife stuck in his throat?"

"It depends. If it hit the carotid artery there would be almost instant unconsciousness. Easily within five to eight seconds, I reckon. Followed by paralysis and then death. Now, is there anything else?"

"Five to eight seconds, Doc? You seem unsure of that."

"Think about it, Detective. It's rare that we have someone with a stop watch in his hand timing the interval between a stabbing and unconsciousness. It's a best guess. Do you have any more questions?"

"Yeah, when do you want to have that arm-wrestling contest?"

"Get out of here, Roark, before I call internal affairs and have them put you in detox to see if you've lost your marbles or on a foreign substance," She smiled for the first time and it was a smile of satisfaction.

Roark saw that and bowed slightly. "I take my leave, quoting Shakespeare".

He was almost to the door when she called back to him. She had already put her glasses on, the ones she used to look at the x-rays. She quickly removed them. "Hey, Roark. I hate to admit it, but you could be right. He might have done it himself. After all, his were the only prints on the knife."

"Yeah. Why did you try to talk me out of it then?"

"Shit. I don't know. I'm not a very religious person but he was a priest. Aren't those guys supposed to be against suicide? Part of me just thinks it makes no sense. Why do it in a confessional? But, you're right. You have to keep your options open. It could have gone down that way."

Roark stopped in his tracks. Holding his chin, he thought, "Okay, let me see if I got this right. His prints are on the knife which usually indicates, correct me if I'm wrong, that he killed himself. If not, you're going to suggest that the guy who really did it wore gloves. So, it's a toss-up. He either did it himself or somebody did it for him and he tried to pull the knife out and that's how his prints got on the knife."

She nodded, "You catch on pretty fast, Roark. My compliments. Now can I get back to work?"

He ignored her, "Okay, he got his hands on the knife. Why wouldn't he have pulled it out of his neck? Is that rigor mortis setting in?"

"No, rigor mortis generally takes longer than that. Maybe thirty minutes or so. My guess is he grabbed the knife but, before he could pull it out, he lost consciousness and his hand fell off the knife. He then became paralyzed and died."

"Thanks, Doc. That helps. Hey, I still want to have that arm-wrestling contest," And he was gone.

57

CHAPTER TWELVE

"How nice to see you, Mr. Roark. I was guessing I might not see you again. And, as I said before, I rather enjoy your questions," The pastor, Father Gregory, seemed to have been transformed, almost like he had inhaled something from the fountain of youth. Contrary to his haggard appearance the night of the murder and during the next visit he, today, looked refreshed.

"I just want to tidy up some things, Father. First of all, I got a visit from Kitty Meadows," he said referring to his notes to make sure he got the name right."

"Ah, yes, Miss Meadows. She's a devout Catholic. Good young woman. Too bad we don't have a whole lot more like her."

"You talked to her about what happened?"

"Yes. I did."

"What exactly did she say to you?

The pastor smiled. It was a mischievous smile like he was enjoying himself.

"She hasn't talked to you?"

"She's talked to me."

"Then why do you need to hear from me what she told me?"

"I need to hear it from you, Father, if you don't mind. Sort of like comparing two versions of what should be the same story," Roark said it with all due emphasis hoping that he had clearly indicated the debate was over.

"You testing her veracity or mine, Inspector? Well, never mind. Here it is. She came to me. The next day, after Sunday. Said she was so sorry to hear Father Tim had been killed. I got the impression she was rather fond of Father Tim."

"In a romantic way?"

"Oh, God no, inspector. Just admiration. A kind of connection between a priest and one of his...well, what should I say? She firmly believed in his counsel."

"She is also very good looking."

"Inspector. Why are you looking for dirt? It's perfectly normal for a young woman to admire a young priest, in a, shall we say, religious way. You know. Strictly platonic."

"Okay. What did she say other than she was sad? Was she shocked? Disbelief?"

"That was it."

"That was it? Of all the parishioners you had in church on Sunday, she was the only one who came all the way to the rectory to tell you how sad she was."

"She mentioned she was there Saturday. In the church. She went to confession."

"So did a few other people."

"She said she saw somebody. A guy. He was kind of mysterious. Wait. What word did she use? Creepy. That was it. She said he was kind of creepy. So, I told her to go see you."

"That's all you told her?"

"Yes, Inspector. That's it. That's all I told her."

"You didn't encourage her to think that he might be the murderer? A pliable young lady, saddened by the murder of her favorite priest? She could easily be talked into thinking the man she saw was the murderer, right?"

"I may have mentioned that it could be a possibility. She really fell to pieces when I said that. I think it scared her more than anything."

"So, you worked on her grief and her fear, talking her into thinking some guy she saw in church must be the murderer?"

"Inspector, please. I have no reason to suggest anything to her. We all grieve about what happened to Father Tim. Like you, we all would like to know what happened and why. It's part of our grieving process. To wonder. And to pray."

"Speaking of what happened and why, let me get back to Father Tim. You said before he was a model priest. Nothing in his past would indicate there was any reason to support or suggest that anyone had any reason to murder him."

"Yes, that's exactly what I said before and I stand by that."

"How long have you known Father Tim?"

The pastor nodded his head in submission, "I see where you're going with this. Okay, you can easily find out so I might as well tell you. He was transferred here just two years ago."

"Transferred? From where?"

"Another parish."

"Which one?"

"I don't recall off hand. I think it might have been San Diego. Yes, some parish in San Diego."

"Isn't that a little unusual?"

The pastor pursed his lips, thinking mightily, "Yes, that is a little unusual. Normally, transfers from one parish to another are within the diocese. San Diego is another diocese. So, yes, that's a little unusual."

"You didn't ask him about it?"

"I had no reason to, Inspector. I was just tickled to death to have an assistant to help me with the work that has to be done here."

"And he never volunteered to tell you?"

"Father Tim was a quiet man. He didn't talk to too much about himself and I'm not a very inquisitive person. Thus, there wasn't a whole lot of conversation about personal stuff. All we ever talked about was church stuff."

"Nothing personal."

"That's what I said, Inspector. Nothing personal. On his days off he did his thing and, on my days off, I did mine."

"Days off? You have days off?"

"Yes, we try to get away one day a week."

"Really? Okay, Father, what does a priest do on his one day a week? Walk around town and try to save souls for Mother Church?"

"I can assure you, Inspector, it's nothing that dramatic. We wear civilian clothes and just go about our business."

"And what kind of business might that be?"

"Visiting relatives. We do have families, Inspector. Fathers, mothers, siblings."

"That's it?"

The pastor threw his hands up in the air. "If you must know, Inspector, Father Tim was a bit of an adventurer. Let's just say he liked to branch out. Do different things."

"Different things. Like what?"

"He surfed. During the summer months he went to the beach and took his surf board with him."

"A surfboard riding priest? Wow. I never would have guessed. What else besides surfing?"

"I think he liked to hike. In the hills. Sometimes in the desert. Palm Springs. That sort of thing."

"Sounds like quite an adventurer our Father Tim was. Let me see if I've got this picture right. Half the time he's out there in his swimming wear, surfing among the guys and gals on the beach and the rest of the time he's roaming around Palm Springs."

"You make it sound like he had a split personality."

"I think it sounds like he yearned for a life other than sitting in a confessional."

"I think your suspicious juices are running away with themselves, Inspector. Priests are not robots. We're normal human beings that have our private lives, things we like to enjoy, just like anybody else. We just limit those things which we are forbidden to indulge in. Father Tim was a young, vibrant man who loved the outdoors but he loved his God and loved serving Him, as a priest. He was a good priest despite what you might be thinking. Let me put it this way, Inspector. Among the priesthood there are priests like me that see the value of the Catholic Church and Christianity and the hope that all that has brought to mankind for two thousand years. I firmly believe there's value there and except for a few things I struggle with I totally accept the Church's teachings and, I hope and pray that, by and large, I've kept my vows as a priest. There are other priests among us that believe in all this on an emotional level. I'm not a man who's given to emotion, Inspector, but there are many priests who are very emotional about being an alter Christ.

Actually, representing Christ here on earth as if he, each priest, were the incarnation of Christ. Father Tim was one of those. Now, does that answer your question, Inspector?" Then he paused like a lawyer who has just completed his closing arguments to a jury.

Roark put his hands together and rested his chin on his fingertips, deep in thought. Then he abruptly stood up and stared down at the pastor who remained placid behind his desk, a look of bewilderment on his face. "Forgive me, Father, I can't stand this anymore. I have to stand. Better yet, I have to pace," Then he put his hands behind his back and paced. "You live in a world where beliefs are what you stake your entire life on. You believe this; you believe that. Whatever's in the Bible you believe. You believe we're all guilty of sin but you don't believe a priest could be guilty of sin. You don't believe a priest would do anything more sinister than go surfing or an innocent walk in the desert. I, Father, live in a different world where beliefs don't mean shit, if you'll pardon the expression. It's all about facts. Verifiable facts and, unless I'm sadly mistaken, you have no facts to go on. You've never saw Father Tim surf and you've never walked with him in the desert. For all you know he might be spending some time with those bikini clad girls on the beach. Or, maybe, he was spending the day with the fair Miss Meadows."

Roark stopped pacing and looked directly at the pastor. He had hoped to see a facial expression that would betray the pastor. It might signal that he was hiding something. Did he touch a nerve mentioning Kitty Meadows? He saw nothing in Father Gregory's demeanor other than a slight spreading of his jowls and lips in a sly smile. Then it was the priest's turn. He erupted. Standing up, he planted his hands on the desk for support.

"Yes, Inspector, I live in a world where I have a belief system. Yes, I trust in the honor of those of my faith who have pledged their love of God and live a life of purity. You live in a world where everyone lies to you. Everyone you come in contact with is a suspect in a crime. They are guilty in your mind until they prove themselves innocent. I feel sorry for you, Inspector Roark, it must be a sad existence yours is to see the bad in everything and everybody you meet. I can see now why you've left Mother Church. You have to have everything proven to you or else you don't believe it. Well, I'm sorry. But not everything can be proven. Some things you have to take on faith. What did the Bible say when Christ appeared to the apostles after he resurrected from grave? He said to Thomas, one of the disciples who, like you, doesn't believe anything unless it's proven to you: 'you believe Thomas because you have seen the holes in my hands but blessed are those who believe without see-ing the proof". So, you can ridicule my belief system if you want. But, right now, from where I'm sitting you haven't proved a thing. All you have is conjecture and you twist things around and try your very best to tarnish the good character of Father Tim and Miss Meadows."

"One thing wrong with what you said, Fa-ther."

"Yes. What's that?"

"You said, and I quote: 'from where I'm sitting you haven't proven a thing'."

"Yes, that's what I said."

"But you're standing."

Shaken, the priest sat down in his chair and looked away.

Roark was angry. He knew he needed to gather himself and act more professionally. "Okay, Father. Look at it from my point of view. Someone murders a priest in the con-fessional. We don't know why. All we know is there must be a history between the two of them. I doubt very much that this guy would just go into to church and just kill whatever priest happened to be in the con-fessional at that time. There has to be more to it than that, some kind of history be-tween the two of them. I need to find that out."

"I wish you the best of luck, Inspector. I really do. And I sympathize with your prob-lem. I'm sorry for getting agitated. I don't know what came over me," His voice trailed off.

"Murder does that to people, Father. You're agitated; I'm agitated. My boss is agitated I haven't an ounce of progress on this case. So, at the moment, I have to tell you that I firmly believe that there's something in Father Tim's past or his recent present that caused him to get on the wrong side of a vicious killer. I can only guess what that might be because you haven't given me the slightest bit of evidence of what Father Tim might really have been up to. But it had to be something. So, I'll leave now but please give it some thought. If you come up with something, you know how to get in touch with me."

"I'll do that, Inspector. I really will."

Roark started to leave then stopped in his tracks, "Wait. Something just occurred to me."

"What's that, Inspector?"

"You priests. I seem to recall from my days when I was a firm believer that you priests go to confession."

"Yes, that is true."

"So, who did Father Tim go to confession to? Do we know?"

"Yes, we do know. It's me."

"You? You hear his confession?"

"Yes. Does that surprise you?"

"Just a little. He works for you. You have some control over his progress and he comes to you and confesses all his sins?"

"That's the way it works, Inspector."

"So, you would know. Because he confessed. Whether or not he was playing hanky-panky with anybody."

"All I know is you need to brush up on your understanding of the law."

"Yeah, I know. You priests have that sanctimonious luxury of not being forced to tell what you hear in confession. Personally, I think that's a bullshit law."

"Until you become president of the United States, Inspector, I'm afraid the law is what it is and my lips are sealed."

"So, tell me why I'm getting this feeling in my gut that you know something you're not telling me," He started to leave then stopped. "Oh, one more thing. I think we need to, once again, ask your parishioners if anybody was there on Saturday and ask them to come forward."

"I thought, Inspector, we already did that when I made my announcement before mass a week ago. Or," he paused. "Did I forget to mention that? Anyway I thought you already had a witness. Why would you need more?"

"Leave that to me, Father, to decide. You preach to your parishioners and I'll do the detective work, okay? I just want to ask again. People sometimes don't always come forward like we'd like them to. Sometimes they need a little prodding. So, now, how are we going to do this? Don't you have something like a bulletin you pass out every Sunday at mass?"

"Yes. But you can't be serious."

"Never more serious. You refuse?"

"Well, of course not. I would never refuse a legitimate request from you, Inspector, it's just that these things have already gone to the printer, a week or so in advance. I can't..."

"You ever heard of an insert? Just type something up and put it inside the bulletin. No, better, I type it up and I'll give it to you tomorrow or the next day."

The priest shook his head slightly, "Oh, dear, that would be a first. An insert telling everybody that Father Tim was murdered and all those people on Saturday who were at confession should come forward. You're going to scare a lot of people, Inspector. Old people who read our bulletin from cover to cover. You're going to really frighten them."

"Would you rather make an announcement at mass?"

Father Gregory nodded with his entire upper torso, "All right, Inspector, you type it, I'll insert it in the bulletin."

Roark came away from the meeting highly agitated and worried. The old priest just seemed to be a bit off from what he expected a priest to be. Could he be hiding something? Roark put that thought away in his memory bank until later when he intended to visit again.

Chapter Thirteen

Tim Hanrahan was the third boy of five boys born to a middle class Irish Catholic family in Long Beach, California. He loved sports and was good at all those that he tried: football, basketball, baseball, tennis. It didn't matter he was a natural athlete.

And a fine, good-looking young man he was. Black hair, strong chin, beautiful blue eyes. His brothers weren't so lucky.

The oldest continued to get in trouble with the Long Beach police department. The second boy followed in his father's footsteps and became an alcoholic while still a teenager. Timothy Hanrahan decided to never follow in the footsteps of his older brothers nor in those of his father. Old man Hanrahan worked on the docks in Long Beach. He left early in the morning, before the boys woke up, came home sweaty and dirty, and began drinking before the boys got home from school. Needless to say, the boys didn't hurry to get home from school. While Tim excelled in sports in grammar school and early in his sports career in high school his two younger brothers didn't inherit any talent in sports. It was as though they came from an altogether different gene pool.

His father died of a massive heart attack in Tim's third year in high school. It was a real shame that he died that early in life because the old man had promised Tim he'd come see him play a baseball game or a football game or whatever game was in season but he never did, never did quite make it. Then he died.

Tim loved his mother. In all the ways his father had failed him, his mother went out of her way to make it up to him, smothering him with hugs and kisses, almost to the point of embarrassment. But there was only so much love to go around and she wanted to be fair and not favor one boy over the other. Though she tried to be fair and give equal love she just couldn't do it. Who could resist not favoring Tim, the all-American kid who didn't get into trouble ever in his life and had so much promise?

There was just one problem. Unlike most kids, Tim had not one, but two dreams and they were mutually exclusive. He had visions of some day being a famous athlete but Tim Hanrahan also fervently wanted to be a priest. He wanted to be a priest for as long as he could remember, ever since his days as an altar boy. As a young lad he was totally mesmerized by the fact that the priest on the altar could actually convert a wafer and some wine into the body and blood of Jesus Christ. That was a powerful thought and, in the end, had more appeal than being an athlete.

If ever there was an expression that characterized a young man it was the old saying; that you can take the boy out of the farm but you can't take the farm out of the boy. Only, in Tim Hanrahan's case, it was more like you can take the priest out of the sports world but you can't take the sports world out of the priest. As a priest he did things differently, much to the consternation of his supervisors. He had a motorcycle that he would ride around the neighborhood, his cassock flying in the wind. People would say, "There goes the bike riding Father Tim." He'd give rides to the kids and they loved him. So, he was different.

As a priest he envisioned himself doing things the way Christ would have done them. His approach was to relate to his flock on an emotional level, on a level as humanly and as compassionately as possible.

It all started with the altar boys. His daily contact with them was a fertile time to get to know them, to grow fond of them as he grew to know them. Knew them by name, he did. It became important to know more about them, as much as he could. Where did they live: what was their family situation? That sort of thing. As much as he could, he would ask them if they had any problems he could help them with, problems that maybe the parents, for whatever reason, failed to solve. They began to tell him their stories. And he would listen. Sometimes, at the end of a heart-breaking story, he'd give the boy a hug, a harmless hug, to be sure. Young girls and their problems were off limits. The nuns could take care of that chore. Father Tim was like the pied piper, the leader of the young boys.

Chapter Fourteen

Roark asked to see the head of records for the diocese of San Diego. It wasn't until he made it clear that his reason for having a meeting was that it was a police matter and involved a murder. Expecting to see another priest he was, instead, ushered in to a young man who, if Roark didn't know better, appeared to be gay. Nattily attired, the young man precisely measured each word and each of his movements. If there remained any doubt, his handshake, limp as it was, told Roark all he needed to know.

"Thank you for seeing me," said Roark, masking his uneasiness and freeing up his hand more quickly than normal.

"You're from the Los Angeles area, Mr. Roark? A little out of your territory, aren't you?" That's when Roark wondered if he might have been just better off calling the office rather than driving over a hundred miles. Easy answer. You call, you can't see the reaction of the person you're talking to. And that was what he wanted to see above all else—the face of whoever made the decision to transfer Father Tim.

"Murder has no boundaries, if I may wax philosophical," Roark retorted.

"My, my. Murder. Really? Sounds awful. Who got murdered and why does that have something to do with the diocese of San Diego?"

"A priest by the name of Timothy Hanrahan. He was serving up near Los Angeles when it happened."

"Oh, dear. A priest murdered. That's nasty business."

"Yes, I suppose that's one way of putting it. Now, San Diego. I understand he came from here before he went to the parish up in Los Angeles."

"Hanrahan. I'm sorry, I don't remember the name. How long ago would this have been?"

"A couple of years."

"Oh, then I'm not the person you need to talk to. I've only been on board for a year."

"Records. Don't you keep records?"

"Of course, we keep records, Mr. Roark. Did you want me to look up something for you?"

"That's exactly why I'm here. To have you look up the records to see under what circumstances Timothy Hanrahan...excuse me...Father Hanrahan was transferred to Los Angeles."

"I'm afraid that's not possible, Mr. Roark."

"You just said you could look it up. Why is that not possible?"

"Because, the records don't elaborate on why a priest is transferred. It's just a simple statement of fact. Nothing more, nothing less. Afraid you drove all this way from Los Angeles for nothing, Mr. Roark."

"Okay, let's not get ahead of ourselves. I'm not done yet."

"Excuse me," the young man answered as sarcastically as he could.

"I'll be blunt," Roark stated. "If a priest was being transferred out of a parish here in San Diego because of, shall we say, some irregular activities, who would sign the order? Who would make the determination?"

"I'm afraid that would be the bishop. Sorry, I'm not the bishop, so I can't help you."

"Is the bishop here, so I might talk to him?" Roark was beginning to show his impatience.

"You said, irregular activities? What are you suggesting, Mr. Roark?"

"It's Detective Roark, if you don't mind and what I'm suggesting is none of your business."

"You think I'm a fool, Detective? I know exactly what you're suggesting and I resent the implication. And I'm sure the bishop will, as well. We have a very clean record here. No pedophile priests here in San Diego, I'm proud to say. All that stuff is somewhere else; not here."

"And you know this how?"

"Trust me; I would know."

"You just said you've only been here a year."

"Only in this job a year. Before that I served Bishop Flannery for five years as his aide."

"Thanks for telling me. Why do I have to drag these things out of you?"

"You need to be precise, Detective, if you expect me to be of any help to you."

Roark felt like shoving a broomstick up the ass of this impertinent young man standing across from him and severely testing his reserve. Good thing there was a desk separating them. "Okay, guy. Let me talk to the bishop."

"Bishop Flannery?"

"Yeah, that one."

"That might be a little difficult, inspector. He died last year and the new bishop decided he didn't need my services so I'm here, stuck in record-keeping."

All the way across the desk from him, Roark could feel the vibrations of jealousy and anger from a young man who had been demoted from the bishop's aide to a clerk. Tough shit, thought Roark.

Driving back to Los Angeles is a beautiful drive up along the famed Pacific Coast Highway, the same highway that goes all the way to Monterrey. Too bad he couldn't enjoy it like most people. He had too much to think about.

He passed Torrey Pines. Oceanside and Camp Pendleton, home of the Marine Corp. Then came long stretches of just plain nothing. Brown hills on his right, the inland side of the highway, and the endless rolling ocean on his left.

His mood changed and his mind drifted off into dreamland. Who can think when there were coastal views like that? Nothing more beautiful than the ocean he thought to himself. Especially when the sun is starting to sink towards the horizon, as it was now. The end of a day. Never to be visited again. Hopefully tomorrow will be a better day, he hoped.

Seeing the ocean this close reminded him of his time in the Navy on the high seas. Carefree days they were then. He hated every moment of it when he was living it but now, looking back, it wasn't so bad. Far less troublesome than what he was dealing with now.

Chapter Fifteen

It had been a long day, driving to San Diego and back, as wasted a trip as it was and he longed to talk to somebody besides an irritating gay guy. He dialed Kitty Meadows' number. It was late but not that late.

"I could meet you somewhere, Mr. Roark. I'd feel a lot better about that. Anywhere other than the police station. That place brings back bad memories."

Roark actually preferred to meet her in her home and this played right into his hands. That way he could see how she lived. Did she live alone? He didn't even know if she lived alone. In any case, that was his modus operandi, to see where people lived and worked, when they were a suspect. God, what a thought that was. Was she a suspect? Technically speaking, like all the others, she was a person of interest. She seemed to know something, more than what she had told him already. How much she knew he intended to find out. What part she might have played in the crime, only time would tell. If it was to be, then it was to be. Beautiful lady or not. In the meantime, he needed to get out of her whatever she knew, whatever she thought she saw. Maybe she knew something about Father Tim that even his boss didn't know. If nothing else, in his sorry predicament at the moment, she was someone to talk to.

She showed up at Starbucks right on time, her hair up in a twisted pony tail on top of her head. It looked like one of those fried onions in a Japanese restaurant. Wearing sweatpants and a matching grey hoodie, she looked totally different than when he saw her before. "I just got out of the shower after running. I'm sorry I didn't have time to get better dressed."

"It's quite all right. You look..." Then he stopped.

"What?" She asked. "What were you going to say?"

"You were running?" He diverted her question. "You run in an outfit like that?

She puckered her nose a little, as if disappointed, "I run every day. Five miles."

"Really? What for?"

"Good health. They say it's good for you. Plus, I think my legs and butt are too big. And running helps."

"They say a lot of things, these people that say things. Did you know joggers only live five years longer than people who don't jog?"

"Really? They keep records on that sort of thing?"

"I have it on good authority. They do."

"Five years. Well, that's worth it, isn't it?"

"Problem is they spend practically all of those years jogging. So, why do it?"

"Oh, dear," she said with a touch of disappointment. "And here I thought I was doing something worthwhile."

"Hey, if it makes you feel good, do it."

"So, what do you think?" She then asked.

"Think? About what?"

"Are my legs and butt too big?"

"Miss Meadows, this is a criminal investigation I'm working on. This is not a social call, if you get my drift."

"Oh, I'm sorry. Stupid me," She looked genuinely rebuked and foolish.

"I was hoping you could give me some more information about the man you saw."

"I told you in the police station two days ago all I know."

"Did you see the sketch artist I asked you to call?"

"Yes. And it was a complete waste of time. He asked me questions and I couldn't answer any of them. So, he told me to go home. He wasn't very nice."

"He works for the police. None of us are very nice. We're always in a bad mood."

"That's awful. How do you live with yourselves? What does your wife think about that?"

"Wife? I'm not married."

"That's a shame. A nice man like you."

"Miss Meadows."

"Could you call me Kitty? I'd feel a lot better. Miss Meadows is so formal. It makes me feel like you're grilling me," Roark drained what was left of his coffee. This conversation was not going well and he wasn't sure why.

"Kitty, the man you saw. Where was he sitting?"

"He wasn't sitting."

"Standing then. Where was that?"

"Oh no, not standing. He was walking the Stations of the Cross. It traces the steps of Christ when he..."

"I'm familiar with the stations, Kitty. No need to explain. So, he was walking the stations of the cross."

"Well, sort of."

"I don't understand."

"He'd walk a little, and then he'd look back at me. Whenever I looked up and caught him looking at me, he'd turn around. Like he didn't want me to see him. It was kind of peculiar what he was doing."

"Peculiar? In what way."

"I watched him. And I'm very certain of this."

"Yes. Certain of what?"

"He wasn't doing the stations of the cross."

"You just said he was. Moments ago. You said he was."

"Did I? Oh, dear. I'm making a mess of things. He looked like he was walking the

Stations of the Cross but he wasn't. I know 'cause he missed several of the stations. There are fourteen of them, Detective, and he missed several of them."

"That gives me something to go on," said Roark in frustration.

"It does?"

"Yeah, it really does. All I need to do now is find a guy who can't count."

"Really?" She wrinkled up her entire face and on her it looked so cute; no so gorgeous and lovable.

"Really," He confirmed, joking at her expense, although she didn't seem to get it or, if she did, she didn't show that she got it. "Let's try something else. How well did you know Father Tim?"

CHAPTER SIXTEEN

Driving home, Roark was totally confused about this case. There had been other tough cases but this one just might be one of the most confusing he'd ever worked on. It was moments like these when he wished he were back being a uniformed patrolman, back when life was simple. You go on duty in the late afternoon and you get off at midnight. During your hours on duty, you drive around; you look for suspicious activity. You see it; you break it up. Or you break a few heads trying. Didn't matter to him which way it turned out. Come midnight, he could go home, have a beer and go to bed and forget anything that happened during the previous eight-hour shift. Ah, the life of a patrolman. If only he could go back.

Then he remembered how his days as a patrolman had turned sour. It was one of those days every patrolman wishes never happens. He and his partner were chasing a very live potential thief who had just robbed a liquor store. Roark was trying his best to keep up with his partner who ran better than him. Out of breath, he got there just in time to see his partner had the robber cornered in a back alley with no escape. But then things turned ugly in a heartbeat. The robber pulled out a gun and aimed it at Roark's partner and fired. Missing Roark's partner with the first shot, the robber fired again, this time hitting Roark's partner in the leg and he went down in a hurry.

In between the two shots, Roark had pulled his revolver when he saw his partner was struggling to get his out of his holster. Roark had the robber in his sights but, for some reason that he could never understand or explain to the review board, he didn't fire it. Fortunately, his partner, even with a bullet in his leg was able to get his revolver out and shoot the guy before he could fire again.

Roark was reminded several times, his failure to fire almost cost his partner his life. This possibility haunted him to no end for several months as he tried to figure out in his own mind why he didn't pull the trigger. Here he was, with his first real legitimate chance to use his revolver and he didn't do it. As if paralyzed, he couldn't pull the trigger. The final result of this nagging self-examination was a determination, a promise he made to himself that, if it ever happened again, he'd do it. He'd pull that trigger. He got promoted before that chance ever came.

Now, he had a 24/7 job. No end to it. No time to forget. A murder had to be solved. No excuses. No time off to be alone with idle thoughts and enjoy the moment. Before he had left for San Diego this morning he'd been called into the chief's office. She was one heck of a woman. Chinese. Imagine that, a Chinese lady as chief detective in a Hispanic neighborhood. Well, not totally Hispanic but there were a lot of them in the hood. She was Chinese but she spoke better English than he did, she so reminded him from time to time. And she wasn't bashful about reminding everybody she was married to an Anglo-Saxon, some political guy downtown. Big deal, thought Roark. But to her, on this particular morning, a murder in her precinct wasn't to go unsolved for very long. Or heads would roll, as she put it. For a Chinese lady she was remarkably well-endowed up top and she stood nearly as tall as Roark. Must have come from ancestors who all played basketball, thought Roark.

He really didn't know what to expect when he was called into her office. Either she was going to ream him out for his lack of progress in the case or she was going to tell him he was going about it in the wrong way. He braced for the worst.

"Do you have any leads at all Detective Roark?" She asked quietly.

"Not really."

"No witnesses?"

"None that are reliable."

"What do you know about the victim?"

"Not much. He was a priest and nobody wants to speak ill of the dead especially when it's a dead priest."

"I suggest then, Roark you better ramp up your investigation and come up with something." Her voice went up an octave. "I'm tempted to take you off the case and give it to somebody else, maybe Culpepper, but I've decided on a better idea. I'm thinking of making him a co-investigator. Maybe it would be better if the two of you worked together to solve this crime. I don't want the Archdiocese of Los Angeles coming down on my head. Do you understand, Roark?"

He shuffled out of her office, his spirits as low as they could get. Culpepper as a partner? No way. Fortunately, he was able to talk her out of that notion, promising better progress than what he had to date. She bought it for now.

Shit, he thought. I better come up with something. He racked his brain. What could he be missing? He went home to his cards and his card table and tried to sort it out, talking out loud as he did.

"I've got a pugnacious pastor who may have had some kind of motive that escapes me for the moment. I've got a female that I don't understand and don't trust. And then there's always her ex-husband, not to mention the mysterious guy in church."

He tossed around in his mind which was the most plausible person who either did the crime or knows more about it than he or she has let on so far?

For better or for worse, he settled on Kitty Meadows who, at this moment, was his primary, if not his best, hope. He looked at his notes; the notes he had made when he had last talked to her. He remembered what his question was and how she had answered it. That was one of the skills that he prided himself on: to be able to remember in great detail conversations he'd recently had with a witness.

Questioning a witness in a public place, like Starbucks, had been totally unorthodox but then this was an unorthodox crime which called for unorthodox methods. Besides, she had clammed up tight, as she explained, from being nervous in a police station and it was her request. So why not? Why not use another venue in which she would be more comfortable and, hopefully, come forward with something?

Still, it was distracting, sitting there with other customers milling about. Every once in a while, he or she would look at them or they would look at Roark and Kitty. Either way, distracting.

CHAPTER SEVENTEEN

"How well did you know Father Tim?" He had asked.

"What a strange question, Detective Roark," she had answered immediately.

"Strange or not, can you answer the question?" He remembered had been his response.

"Can I call you by your first name? It would make things a lot easier for me?"

"Okay. It's Sebastian and if you call me Sea Bass I'm going to throw up. I'll throw up all over this table."

"Throw up. Oh, dear. Why is that?"

"It's a long story and I'm running out of time. How well did you know Father Tim?"

"Sebastian. That's a nice name. Unique. I like that. Father Tim? I talked to him a number of times. About religion."

"Religion? Anything in particular? Religion is a pretty broad subject."

She looked away; her face sad, "All right, Sebastian. I'm divorced and the church frowns on divorce. We talked about that. Does that answer your question?"

All of a sudden, as if by a magical transformation, Kitty Meadows had taken on an entirely new personality. Not as nervous; a little more antagonistic when she wanted to be. It gave Roark cause to really reevaluate her, to realize he might not have her completely in a one-dimensional box.

"You got divorced. Okay. So, what was there to talk about with Father Tim?"

"You're getting awfully personal, Sebastian. Does this really have anything to do with the murder?"

"Let me make that determination, Kitty. That's what I'm trained to do."

"You're trained to delve into people's personal lives? What kind of police work is that?"

"It may have a bearing on something."

"I think the only thing it has a bearing on is my personal life and that, Sebastian, is none of your business."

"Okay, Kitty. You can get belligerent if you want, and I can have you taken down to the police station again and we do it there. I thought, meeting here, you were going to be more cooperative."

She looked away, a far-off look, like she was searching for something. Then she blurted it out, "I was a victim of abuse for two years. He made me do things I didn't want to do. It was awful. I couldn't leave our apartment without him questioning where I was going and who I was going to see. If I was late coming home from work fifteen minutes, he would question me. It was awful." Then she started to cry, softly, so as not to disturb or alert other people sitting around in the coffee house.

Roark was taken back. He wasn't quite expecting this. Now he felt like a horse's ass. Tough he was; but cruel, no, "I'm sorry, Kitty, I had no idea. I'm really sorry. Can you stop crying? People are going to wonder if I'm abusing you. Plus, this is getting us nowhere."

She dried her eyes with the sleeve of her hoodie. Very unladylike, thought Roark. But, without a napkin on the table, what else could she do? He didn't have a handkerchief to give her, like the heroes always do in the movies. He'd never carried a handkerchief in his entire life.

Her composure restored, she continued, "When I first told Father Tim what had happened, he actually got out of his chair and came around his desk and came over to me and hugged me. I was totally surprised. I didn't think priests were supposed to do that sort of thing. You know, hug ladies the same age as him. Anyway, I felt really self-conscious and totally awkward and was thinking of pulling away from him but it just felt so good, to have somebody hug me. So, I didn't stop him. I just let it happen."

"You didn't pull away so he just kept hugging you?"

"He kissed me on the cheek."

"What? Are you kidding?"

"No, I'm not. I was shocked. I didn't know what to say."

"Then what happened?"

"Why nothing. That was it. He felt awkward. I guess he felt ashamed. Maybe he wasn't supposed to do that, you know, kiss a lady on the cheek. He was back behind his desk before I knew it. Then he apologized."

And that's all he could remember from Starbucks other than paying the bill and watching people look at them as they left the restaurant. Then she took off in her running suit. He went to find his car.

It had truly been a long day; threats from his Chinese supervisor, a drive to San Diego and back, a total waste of time talking to a belligerent gay guy and finding out nothing, and then a tearful meeting in a coffee house. What on earth was he to make of the things Kitty Meadows had gone on to tell him. Tomorrow, he was determined to solve a more important problem. Somehow, someway, he had to get Culpepper out of the office and out of his hair, making it difficult for the commissioner to saddle him with a partner. But how could he pull that off? Putting a bullet between his eyes was the best way but perhaps a bit harsh. Maybe put something in his coffee that will give him diarrhea for a couple of weeks.

CHAPTER EIGHTEEN

In his apartment, though space was at a premium, he managed to set aside a spot on a card table where he could lay out his investigation. Three by five-inch cards each contained a person of interest and the victim. On each card was written certain key facts. In so doing he was able to see the situation more visually rather than just lay awake at night and try to visualize everything in his head. First thing, in the morning, he added to his card collection all the things he had learned the previous day. His goal was to make more notes on the cards and juggle them around like he usually did each day of an investigation.

Alongside each person of interest, he would place a card which showed why that person might be guilty of the crime. What was that person's motivation? What was that person's alibi? Things like that. The display sure helped. The reason he didn't like doing all this at the station was there were too many eyes watching him. Too many people sticking their collective noses in his business.

He started with the pastor. Motive? Hard to know. Something in the pastor's past. What could it be? Hard to know. Was the old pastor a pedophile? Probably not now but maybe years ago? He noted on the card. But then not very likely, he noted on the card. Why? The good pastor was a former Marine. He remembered that part of one of his conversations.

"Were you ever in the service, Father?"

"Marine corps, Inspector. I'm a former Marine."

Roark had smiled, "What I hear is there are no former Marines. Once a Marine, always a Marine, is what I hear?"

"I'm a priest now, Inspector. What about you, while we're on that subject? You ever been in the service?"

"Navy."

"Ah, the Navy. You guys drove the bus and we did all the fighting. You know what Marines call sailors?"

"I'm sure it's very complimentary," said Roark sarcastically.

"Pussies. Pardon my language but, like you said, once a Marine always a Marine."

"Just guessing, Father. You ever did any boxing?"

"You are good, Inspector. Very good. I'm impressed," The priest's face lit up in a broad smile, either amplifying his admiration for Roark's talents in figuring people out or he was just having a gas attack.

"It's my job. To sort of figure people out."

"Yes, I did a lot of boxing in my youth and I thought I was pretty good at it until a black Marine whipped my ass in the ring. Very humbling it was but, looking back, I think that guy did me a favor. Once the cuts mended on my face I never boxed again."

So, to be clear, the pastor wasn't *that* old and being an ex-Marine meant he could be dangerous. Dangerous enough to kill someone. But a pedophile? Not very likely. Roark dismissed that idea. It must be something else.

The mysterious man in church, the man who, in Kitty's words pretended to walk the Stations of the Cross but mess it up because he couldn't count to fourteen? Is that it? He just couldn't count to fourteen or was he terribly distracted by Kitty Meadows staring at him? Straight line. So, he might be a perfectly innocent skirt-chaser, if there is such a thing. Or, he might be the murderer. If so, why? What motive? Some grievance he had against lovable Father Tim? What could that possibly have been? Once again, the word pedophile came to mind. Father Tim, a pedophile? Didn't match what he now knew of him. Too much of a lady's man, for his own good apparently. Kissing Miss Meadows on the cheek? Not the sort of thing that would make you think he could have been a pedophile.

That leaves Father Tim and Kitty Meadows. He recalled an expression that, seemed, at this juncture, to be so appropriate. Where there's smoke, there's fire. No question about it, in his mind anyway, romantic love and rejection has caused more problems than all the wars combined. Father Tim and Kitty Meadows. It had to be the answer. What did she say, after she said he kissed her on the cheek?

"He was red-faced. And he apologized."

"I told him it was all right but he continued to apologize. If the truth be told, Sebastian, what he did, it made me feel really good for a few seconds. Actually," she said, wistfully recalling that day, "it made me feel really good all the rest of the day and the next several days after that. For the first time in a long time it made me feel like a woman again instead of a piece of rotten meat like I had felt before that."

Roark was embarrassed to admit that he answered in a most unprofessional way. "You're certainly no rotten piece of meat, Kitty. In fact, I'd say...well, never mind. I understand what you're saying and what else can I say? Father Tim was a caring kind of guy."

"A very caring kind of guy," she added.

What else did she say? He tried to remember. Didn't matter the precise words, or did it? He asked her, "Did you see him again? One on one, I mean."

"Oh, yes, several times."

"Several times, and this was because?"

"Like I told you Sebastian, he was helping me. Is there something wrong that?"

"That depends. Depends on what kind of help he was giving you."

Then she told him the whole story. "I suppose you wondered why I was so nervous when we first met, back there in the police station."

"The thought crossed my mind."

She again looked away, possibly trying to remember something or maybe, he supposed, thinking of what things to leave out.

"After the divorce. I went to my ex's apartment to reclaim something he had stolen from me. He promised me on the phone he'd give it to me if I came to his apartment. I guess I was foolish enough to believe him and think he'd actually let me have it."

Roark remembered she sniffled a little, fighting the temptation to tear up again. He remembered thinking she was either awfully sensitive or putting on an act for his benefit.

"It was a statue of the Blessed Mary. His mother had given it to me, before she died. I think he thought she had given it to us instead of to me and felt he had a right to it. I didn't know it was missing until weeks later when I went to try to find it in my things. Anyway, he got really wild and crazy and accused me of all sorts of things. Then I saw the statue. It was on his coffee table in his living room. It was a beautiful statue, Sebastian, and I wanted it. And he knew that. I think he used it as...what would you call it? It was a trap and the statue was the bait."

"Like putting cheese in front of a mouse?"

"Yes, something like that. Anyway, he told me if I wanted it to go get it. I guess I was foolish into thinking that's all I needed to do," then, as if on cue, she started to tear up again. It was all very convincing.

"If you want," Roark had offered. "We can skip this part."

"No," she said, drying her eyes again with the sleeve of her hoodie. "I want you to know what happened. Maybe you'll understand. He grabbed me. Just as I was reaching for the statue. He half tore my top off and was trying to, you know, get his hands on me. I did the only thing I could think of. I know I shouldn't have done it but I did. And I'm not sorry. He deserved it."

"Kitty. I'm not sure what you're telling me. He grabbed you and he tried to have his way with you? What did you do that was so wrong? Help me out here."

"I hit him with the statue of the Blessed Virgin Mary."

"Oh, my God, Kitty. As a police officer I have to question this but, as a man, I have to applaud your courage. I'd say the guy deserved it. You say it was a statue?"

"Well, not a big statue, no. It was more like a figurine, you know, like twelve inches or so. But it was solid. Not exactly like glass. More like solid marble, I guess. He was bleeding pretty bad and he went to his knees. He asked me to call 911. I put a towel around his head to try to stop the bleeding and, before we knew it, the police were there and a paramedic and... It was just awful."

"Sounds a little crazy. But in my mind the guy got what he deserved but I don't see what this has to do with you being nervous at the station and all the rest of it."

"What came next was he accused me of assaulting him with the Blessed Virgin and I accused him of sexually assaulting me. I had to go to the police station and file my report and then I had to answer a lot of questions. And it was awful. They actually accused me of provoking him. Can you believe that?"

"Why would that be?"

"They said it was the way I was dressed. That I, well, you know. I led him on. It was crazy the way they were accusing me. So now you see why I hate police stations? And, up until the time I met you, I wasn't too fond of policemen or anybody working with the police."

This latest part of her sad story Roark had to truly question in his mind. In law enforcement, almost any place you go, officers are taught to treat the victim with respect. To avoid being judgmental. So, this part of the story just didn't wash, in his mind, as he let it roll around in his head but then he had to admit. Anything's possible and why would she lie about a thing like that?

"Were you dressed in a provocative way?"

She hesitated for a split second, "I guess I wanted him to see what he was going to be missing."

"I'll take that as a yes," He remembered taking a deep breath just to clear the air and his own brain which was getting more confused by the minute. "Okay, Kitty. I get it. You have had some bad memories."

Listening to her story, he began to seriously wonder, as was a policeman's habit, whether or not she was telling the truth. Over the years, he'd found that questioning people fairly soon after an incident, they'd have one version of the story. Questioning them a week later, they'd invariably have another version of the story and no two people, viewing the same scene, would ever remember it exactly the same. That's why investigations take so long and why we have court trials, thought Roark. Anyway, what has all this got to do with Father Tim?

Was she making it up, lying to her teeth, or did it really happen just the way she had been telling him? He intended to find out, if he could. It was just going to take a while to

sort it out and, surely, pay her another visit.

So, now he had three real suspects. A
priest who had some weaknesses and a bit
of a violent past, a mystery guy who faked
doing the stations of the cross and now,
ranking right up there, near the top, a
woman who could slam a marble figurine
into the side of a guy's head.

Chapter Nineteen

It was soon after she first met Father Tim and had told him about the mistreatment she had endured and he had hugged and kissed her on the cheek that she called him again. At first, she was embarrassed for him and maybe a little embarrassed for herself. Or, maybe it wasn't embarrassment at all but more like wanting to relive it again and seeing him certainly refreshed that sweet memory, how good it had felt at the time. Maybe, she hoped, in her wildest fantasy, he would hold her again and she wished with all her might he would.

No, that can't be, she shook herself to reality. He's a priest. I'm going to have to go to confession and confess that thought. Still, she had questions and he was the only one who could answer those questions.

"Father, it's me. Kitty. Kitty Meadows. Remember? I hate to bother you with my problems but I was wondering if we could talk again. I have some more questions and I don't know where else to turn.

"Miss Meadows," Father Tim said softly. "Maybe it's best if you talked to the pastor.

He can help you. Under the circumstances, I..."

"You don't want to talk to me? But I need your help and... I can't talk to Father Gregory. He just seems too, I don't know, too harsh. Not easy to talk to. Not like you."

"Okay, Miss Meadows."

"Please call me Kitty. Miss Meadows makes me sound old and like a stranger you've never met before."

"Okay. Kitty. I'll help you, if I can but I don't think we should meet here at the rectory. How about I pick you up in my car in front of the library tomorrow. It's my day off but we can talk. How about around lunch time? We could go to lunch and talk."

"I work until five o'clock, Father. Could we meet after that?"

When she got into the car his senses were flooded with her scent, a very nice perfume. She had obviously gone home and changed clothes or she had driven every man at work crazy the way she was dressed.

"We might as well get something to eat. We can talk in a restaurant as easily as any place else," he said. "Let's drive a few miles. I know of a nice restaurant where we can go and not be seen by anybody in the parish."

"You make it sound like we're a couple of criminals, or, worse yet, a couple about to ...well, you know. Never mind, I said that. I didn't mean anything by it. I was just babbling. I'm terribly sorry."

"It's okay. I just don't think it's a good idea. People could draw the wrong conclusions and then we'd both have to answer to Father Gregory."

Once seated in the restaurant, and much to her surprise, Father Tim ordered a martini. She ordered a glass of white wine. "Might as well enjoy ourselves while we're at it," he said.

"This is a nice restaurant," was all she could think of to say. "You've been here before? You've brought other people you're helping here?"

"You said you had questions, my dear."

"That sounds nice. My dear. That sounds very nice. It's been a quite a while since anybody's called me, my dear."

"I call everybody, my dear. Well, not the men who I talk to but, yes, all the ladies. I call them, 'my dear.' Now, you said you had questions."

She took her sip of the white wine and wrinkled her nose at its strength and taste, "I don't drink very often. Seldom, if ever. This is a real treat."

"Questions, Kitty?"

"Oh, yes. Let me see. Where do I begin? It's kind of embarrassing."

"Remember, I'm a priest. No need to be embarrassed."

She paused deep in thought and, absentmindedly, took another sip of wine, "After the divorce and that awful incident when

I hit him over the head with the Virgin Mary, I started thinking. Now what? What do I do with rest of my life? I'm a divorced woman with no children and my parents are deceased. I couldn't sleep. All I could think of was how awful my marriage had been and how it ended. It took me a couple of weeks to realize that I needed to change my life. I couldn't go on like this. It had only been two, three weeks but I knew it just wasn't going to get any better until I changed my life and started all over again."

Father Tim smiled, "You're not thinking of becoming a nun, are you?"

"Oh God, no, Father. I was thinking the only way to put all these bad parts in my life out of my mind would be to get married again. To have someone love me, to care about me. Without that, I'd always think of those two awful years I spent with that man."

"Oh," Father Tim said with relief. "You had me worried there for a moment."

"You don't think I'd make a good nun, Father?"

Father Tim shook his head, "No, I didn't mean it that way. You might make a fine nun but I'm thinking that's not what you want and so no point in thinking of that."

"So, that's my question," she said. "How would I get married in the church a second time if I'm divorced? Father Gregory said that's not possible."

"You asked him already?"

"Yes. Just once. In confession."

"What did he say?"

"He said the church has very strict rules about that sort of thing. Then I asked him if that meant I can never have sex."

"And he said?"

"He said I should know how the church feels about sex outside of marriage."

"So, I said that means I can't get married and I can't have sex and none of this was my fault and that's not fair."

"Did he offer any other suggestions?"

"He said that might all be true that it was not my fault but it's God's will and I just have to accept it."

Father Tim looked at the waitress who was asking him if he wanted another drink. "I think I'd better switch to ginger ale since I'm driving. Kitty? Do you want another one?"

She didn't even look at him. Concentrating on a nearby table, she just shook her head in the negative.

Father Tim said, "It's not quite as cut and dried as Father Gregory would lead you to believe. Actually, there are remedies. Kitty?"

He noticed she wasn't listening, still distracted by whatever it was that had caught her eye, "What are you doing? Why are you staring at that other table?" And then he saw it. Sitting at that table, near theirs, was a priest in full priest uniform and a gentleman across from his whose face Father Tim couldn't see.

"What is it, what's the fascination?" He asked again.

This woke her up from her trance. "He's been looking over here from time to time. He's been looking at us. Do you know him?"

"The priest? No. I don't know him. Let's hope he doesn't know me. That's the last thing I need. Just don't look over there. Maybe he'll stop looking or he'll finish dinner and go away."

"You were saying there are remedies?"

"Yes, but let me ask you. Were you married to this guy in the church? Was he a Catholic?"

"He said he was but he didn't go to church very often. So, I'd have to go alone. He always had some excuse why he couldn't go."

"Were you married in the church?" Father Tim repeated his question.

"Of course. Where else, Father?"

"Agreed. Where else? But I had to ask."

"Why does that matter?"

"The Catholic Church does not believe in divorce. It's rooted in the Bible: 'Whatever God has joined together, let no man cast asunder'. But the Church feels that an annulment should be granted in certain circumstances. In those cases, the marriage is decreed invalid ab initio."

She wrinkled her nose at the Latin phrase.

"Ab initio. It's Latin for 'from the beginning'. It basically means the marriage never happened."

"I like that idea. It never happened. That would be wonderful. Can we do that? I mean can I do that? Or do you do that?"

"It's not up to me. It's more a process that is handled downtown at the Archbishop's office."

"Oh. That sounds complicated. I have to go downtown to do this?"

"Well, we start here. I would start the process."

"Would you? That would be wonderful."

"Well, don't get your hopes up, Kitty. It gets a little complicated."

"Oh. Complicated how?"

"I would need to interview you and your husband."

"Jerry? You'd have to talk to him? Oh, God. That would be awful."

"He would have to be willing to testify that, well, this is where it gets complicated. He'd have to be willing to testify that he never completed the marriage vows or possibly never intended to complete the marriage vows. It's sort of like a legal contract. If one party doesn't fulfill his or her obligations or never intended in the first place to fulfill those obligations then there's no contract."

"Ab initio?" She said, grinning. "See, I've followed everything you've said."

"Yes, ab initio. We need him to testify."

"That sounds great. There's just one problem, I don't think he would. He still hates me for what I did to him."

"Hitting him over the head with Blessed Virgin?"

"That and divorcing him. Telling the judge how abusive he was."

"I'll talk to him and see if I can persuade him. I think I can appeal to his sense of decency."

"I don't think he has any sense of decency."

"We'll see. I can only try. That's the least I can do. Until then I can ask you. Did you intend to keep your marriage vows and did you consummate the marriage."

"I did. I think I did. I was in love, at the time. I guess I was just foolish though."

"You were in love but you were foolish? Isn't that the way love usually works? It makes fools of us all? So, I'm told, mind you. I have no personal experience with that."

"You've never been in love, Father?"

"Kitty, please this is not about me," He paused to let her absorb his rebuke. "I've been in love, yes. With God. The church. That's enough for me."

"That just seems so sad. If you don't mind me saying so."

"You mentioned you were foolish. I'm not sure I understand what you meant by that."

She pondered then said, "In the beginning he was a little crude, a little rough around the edges and I told him it bothered me. And he said he'd try to do better."

"Did he?"

"Not really."

"Why didn't you break it off then?"

"I tried a couple of times but then he pleaded with me, promising he'd change."

"Did he?"

"A little. Enough I could tell he was trying. Then..."

"What?"

"Then he asked me to marry him. He said once we were married, he'd feel more confident that I was really his, that I belonged to him."

Father Tim winced, "The church teaches that a woman should respect her husband and be dutiful and, I suppose, obedient but it sounds like he had more than that in mind."

She nodded her head, "I guess I thought, after the wedding, when he knew I belonged to him things would get better."

"Did they?"

"At first, I think they did. I just don't remember any more. But then he went back to being his usual self and things just got worse."

Now it was time for Father Tim to look away, avoiding eye to eye contact with her as if, eye to eye, there would be an exchange he wanted to avoid. He wanted so badly to console her but he was also a bit disappointed in her that she had such low self-esteem as to accept something that wasn't quite right only under the desperate hope that they would get better.

Then she said, "Oh, no. He's coming over."

Before he could understand what she was referring to he was there, the priest from the other table, standing at their table, smiling, "I hate to barge in on you like this but I just had to come over and say it. You two make a lovely couple. There, I've said it. Sorry to have bothered you two. I'll leave you now." And he was gone as suddenly as he had appeared.

Father Tim and Kitty sat for a moment in total silence neither knowing what to say. Then they both burst out laughing.

Chapter Twenty

"Hey, Sea Bass, looks like we're going to be working together after all," Culpepper was all smiles, like a cat that had just caught a mouse. Roark looked totally confused. "She didn't tell you, our China Doll?"

Roark shook his head negatively.

"Well, doesn't matter," announced Culpepper triumphantly with an amazing tone of finality. "I guess our China Doll thought two heads are better than one, right, Sea Bass?"

"You've got to be fucking kidding me. When did you hear this? Never mind. It doesn't matter."

"Hey, Sea Bass, stop fussing. Look at it this way. I get to help you out. How bad is that?"

Roark didn't answer.

Culpepper continued. "Hey, look, Sea Bass, now that we're working together, I think you should show me a little more respect and stop calling me 'Jackass'. Would that be too much to ask for? Sea Bass? Did you hear me?"

"Yeah. Yeah, I heard you. What? What did you want?"

"I asked that you stop calling me 'jackass'. Since I'm your new partner and all that. I think I deserve a little more respect."

Still in a daze, Roark mumbled. "Of course. I understand. From now on I'll call you 'asshole'. That's a bit more accurate and less degrading to the animal kingdom."

"Hey, Sea Bass, that's not fucking funny.

"Why...." Culpepper choked. "Why are you always putting me down? It's not fucking funny any more."

"You know what's not fucking funny? You want to know why I'm always putting you down?" Roark stood up, shaking. "I don't work well with people who don't take this fucking job seriously. You just do it to draw a paycheck. I do it because I think I'm accomplishing something. When you do it, you think you can joke and fuck around. When I do it, I'm all business."

"Jesus, Sea Bass. I didn't know. I mean, I didn't know you felt that way," A meaningful silence followed as both men let their temperatures cool down. Culpepper was the first to speak. "I just act that way for the fun of it. I actually love this job but I always felt like I had to be cool. You know what I mean? It's not easy keeping up with guys like you."

"What are you talking about?"

"I've always admired the way you work, Roark. I guess I was kind of intimidated, that's all. I knew I couldn't compete with you and it bothered me so I just joked around like I didn't care."

"Huh?"

"But I do care."

Roark sat in silence. Then he looked out the window, gathering his thoughts, looking at times as though he might not have any thoughts to gather. Then he said, "All right. Culpepper."

"Roy. Call me Roy, Sebastian."

"Okay, okay," Almost as if he were about to choke on the name, he said it. "Roy. Roy, it is then."

"Can we smoke the peace-pipe then, Sebastian? Start over?"

Roark grunted his consent.

"Good," Culpepper answered. "You know I think you and I, we might make a perfect team. Like the dynamic duo. You know. Batman and Robin."

"Huh?" Roark asked absentmindedly.

"Yeah, with your brains and my brawn, we make quite a pair.

Right after lunch, he went in to see the commissioner. Each and every time he was in her office, he was amazed at how beautiful she was, in an Oriental sort of way. Not that he was affected by it. Just surprised by it. Narrow Oriental eyes, perfectly toned golden skin, slender build. Sensuous. Didn't hurt that her ancestors may have played basketball. At five foot ten inches, she was quite an authority figure. He much preferred, to be honest, an older, beer drinking, big-gutted man with a cigar hanging out of his mouth as the commissioner, but there was nothing he could do about it.

"You found out?" She said. He shrugged his shoulders. "I was going to tell you first but I bumped into Culpepper in the hallway and it just blurted out."

"It's okay. I don't care."

"Are you going to pout now, Roark, or accept the help I'm giving you?" Roark said nothing. "You know, Roark, that's always been your problem. You're a bulldog investigator and that's good but you never ask for help. What is it? Pride?" She paused to let her words sink in. "You know your job. It's to investigate and you do a damn fine job of it. Mine is to manage this whole team. We all work together in this building. But you? You're a lone wolf. Never ask for help. And while I'm at it I might as well tell you that you have a reputation. A reputation for not being good at taking orders." She paused again, waiting for a reaction. Seeing repressed anger behind his stoic expression, she softened her voice. "Aside from that you're a pretty good cop," she said, smiling infectiously.

"I'm aware of my shortcomings, Commissioner. I'll try to do better in the future but, I have to say, I work better alone."

"That may be but your success working alone seems to be slipping a bit. I hear you got no reliable witnesses, no motive, no nothing.”

“You've been listening to Culpepper?” Roark was fuming.

“Yes, I have. He's been filling me in on a daily basis.”

“His idea or yours?”

She ignored his question. Changing the subject, she began to pontificate. “Like I said before. I don't want the Catholic Archdiocese of Los Angeles coming down on my head so you'll work with Culpepper or I'll take you off the case. This is not a simple murder. This has the potential for being a serial killing. Yes, you heard me right. A serial killing. A copy cat, whatever you want to call it. Another nut job out there sees we haven't solved this case: he gets the idea in his head to do the same thing. We need this case to be solved.”

“I get that.”

“So, I'm going to give you a suggestion. You know we quite often use professionals as criminal profilers to help us. I suggest you go visit the one we use most often. Culpepper has his name. You two should go pay him a visit.”

As he was about to leave, she stopped him, “Roark. I forgot something.”

He paused, fearing the worst. But then what could be worse than being chewed out and saddled with an idiot like Culpepper for a partner.

"HR tells me you haven't had a physical exam since you were a patrolman. Not good, Roark. Not good for your health."

"I feel fine."

"Get the physical, Roark. I'll give you a couple of weeks."

Back in his office he cleared his mind of all other thoughts other than the decisions needing to be made. The first was simple. He and his new partner, do they ride in the car together wherever he goes, do they walk together, talk together, or go their separate ways during the day and share information at the end of the day? Do they go to the bathroom together?

No way was Roark going to invite Culpepper to his apartment to view the card table layout. He'd simply tell him what he felt he was entitled to know and that was that. Problem was this. It was no longer up to him. Whatever he did or didn't do to cooperate and include with his new partner was going to go directly to the commissioner faster than a fart going through the trousers. He shrugged his shoulders. The first order of business was to visit the police shrink, as he was inclined to call him. Lot of good this is going to do, Roark thought. But, can't fight city hall.

He said to Culpepper, "Let's go Jack... I mean Roy. We got to see a shrink."

"They want you tested, Sebastian?"

"Let's go, Roy boy, before I shoot you right here in the office."

121

Chapter Twenty-One

They went to the office of a guy the Commissioner had suggested they see. He was a short, squat man, with a square head and beady eyes. What hair he had on top of his head looked like wild prairie grass. He invited them to sit down opposite his desk. He was the department's expert on psychoanalyzing criminals, breaking down in precise terms, how they think, what motivates them, what they might do next, and why they might do it. That sort of thing.

"How can I help you gentleman? Marvin Schofield at your service," and he smiled one of those smiles that could have been described as a shit eating grin, as Roark had heard it described thousands of times in the Navy.

Roark took an immediate disliking to the man. It wasn't just that he had a square head and beady eyes; it was his demeanor and an unmistakable look of superiority. Pretending to be affable and helpful his eyes told a different story. He had what Roark called "evil eyes". Roark was also bothered by the fact that, unlike his own desk, this man's desk was completely clean of any

knick-knacks or material of any sort whatsoever. Except, behind him, on a matching
brown credenza sat a picture of what had to
be his wife. The photo showed her to be
reasonably good-looking and friendly. Easily
too good looking for a guy with a square
head and beady eyes. Two teenage children
with plastic smiles stood on either side of
her. None of them looked all that happy,
more like they'd just eaten some rotten fish.

Back to business, he thought. Taking his
time to mention everything, Roark laid out
all the facts as he knew them to be. Every
once in a while, he'd pause to see the reaction on Schofield's face. To see if it changed
from one fact to another, but it never did.
The man repeated the shit eating grin of a
smile like it was glued onto his face.

"Hmmnnnnn..." Was the only response
they got from Schofield when Roark was
done. Then, "That's quite a little problem
you have there. Not much to go on."

Culpepper spoke up before Roark could
object, "Do you think, from what you know
now, that the priest could have killed himself?"

The man with the square head looked
down at his desk then back over the top of
Roark and Culpepper like he was delivering
a speech. He crossed his fingers in front of
his face, "It's entirely possible. Two things
come to mind whenever analyzing suicidal
tendencies. One, depression, the other,

desperation. If a person is threatened severely enough and there's no way out, sometimes, depending upon the person, they may see death as the only option. It would have to have been something fairly serious that the priest would have been facing. Disgrace maybe. Being defrocked of his priesthood. Maybe he committed a crime that was going to be reported. It's hard to say especially when we have so little to go on."

"You mentioned depression," Roark asked.

"Yes. That's usually a more common cause as to why someone decides to end it all. Depression, it's a powerful force. When someone sees no joy in life, no reason to continue living, no one to turn to for help. That's usually a downhill cycle that accelerates as each day turns out to be like all the others with nothing but despair. Pretty soon, the idea of ending the torture that this person feels is more powerful than the instinct to preserve life. That's what it's all about. The torture becomes so great that it trumps the natural instinct to preserve life because life, at this stage of the game, is not enjoyable, and hardly bearable. The alternative then seems a better solution. And remember the person suffering from this kind of thought process is no longer himself. He's not thinking clearly. He's frantically looking for solutions to his problems and there's no door to open, no window to look out of. He feels surrounded by doom. Sooner or later he wants to end it all, thereby putting an end to his suffering."

Roark and Culpepper both sat silently, in awe that such a display of intricate details could come out of a diminutive man with a square head and beady eyes.

Then Schofield asked, "Any idea what may have been troubling our victim?"

Racing to speak before Culpepper had a chance, Roark responded, "From what I gather, he may have been in love."

"A priest? You mean with a woman?" He quickly added. "Or, an idea, a crusade?"

"A woman. A very beautiful woman, I might add," As he said the words, Roark was surprised those words came out of his mouth and was further surprised that it solicited from him pangs of jealousy, an emotion he'd never felt before in his entire life.

"I see," said the square headed man. "That surprises me but, then again, it doesn't surprise me. Knowing what I know about the Catholic Church I'd have to say it doesn't surprise me at all."

"Could you run that by me again?" Roark asked for clarification.

"In my view, the Catholic Church is an organization that has become so big and so twisted it's hard to put it into simple terms. It continues to cling to beliefs and laws out of the dark ages that were, even at that time, a clear perversion of the Bible."

"Pardon me for interrupting," Roark said. "But, is this a subject you feel qualified to discuss? I mean we're here to discuss a murder, not the Catholic Church."

"Before I got my degree in psychology, Inspector, I had a master's degree in religion. Trust me. I know all of the world's so-called leading religions. I know all their weaknesses and all their strengths, such as they might be, why they appeal to certain people, and not to others."

"You seem to be particularly down on the Catholic Church. You got some kind of axe to grind?"

"Inspector, I thought you were here to hear what I have to say. To help you solve a crime. Please don't question my credentials. Otherwise, we have nothing else to talk about. Trust me. I know what I'm talking about. If you know your Bible you know it says it right there. By their actions you will know them. The phrase "false prophets" readily comes to mind. There's no question in my mind, the Catholic Church is a perversion of what the Bible has laid out for us. It is the consummate false prophet."

"That's an awfully harsh statement to make and I suspect rather an exaggerated accusation at best."

"My, my, Inspector. Did I touch a nerve? You seem inclined to defend the Church?"

"Old habits, I guess. Sometimes, they're hard to break. Anyway, let's get back to what you said. False prophets or no, what would drive a man, a priest, to suicide?"

Schofield ran on and on touching on various theories about suicide. It sounded like a rehash of what he had already said before and Roark was quickly losing patience.

"Yeah, yeah, yeah. But here is this priest, in a confessional. Why would he suddenly decide to do himself in?"

"I never suggested he would, Inspector. I was merely answering your question. What could possibly have driven him to do it?"

"You don't think he did it then?"

"Let's suppose, inspector, your young lady, Miss Meadows? Was that her name? She went to confession and told him she was going to turn him in for fornicating with her. Think of it, Inspector. He's shamed before his family, his friends, all the people who relied upon him to teach them God's will. He's kicked out of the priesthood. Well, it's possible, don't you think?"

"Where did he get the knife? Did she bring it with her to confession?"

"Inspector Roark. You're toying with me now. My job is to deliver to you the possibilities that the human mind is capable of thinking. I leave the details to you."

As he was sitting there listening to Schofield pontificate, his mind wandered and the same thought suddenly occurred to him, as before. If Father Tim did himself in, he would have had to be right-handed, would he not? God, how stupid of me, thought Roark, to not have pinned that down. That little omission of investigatory process he vowed he would remedy, first chance he got. If, by chance, he was left-handed, it had to be murder.

"Let's talk about murder, Mr. Schofield. Or should I call you Doctor Schofield?"

"There's no need to be formal here, Inspector. We're all in this together, are we not? Please, call me Marvin."

"Marvin. Forgetting suicide for the moment, what would bring a person to commit a crime like that?"

"Passion, I suppose. Oh, I shouldn't say it that way. It makes me sound like I'm guessing. It's definitely a crime of passion, something very personal. Guns and bombs are destructive weapons, to be sure, but they're not personal. A knife to the neck is very personal. Whoever did this had a real hatred of the priest, the Catholic Church, or both."

"Any theories of what might, specifically drive a man to do that? What are we talking about here? Theology? Something else?"

"I can tell you what I think in one word, Inspector. Pedophilia. It has all the trappings of a man who was taken advantage of by a priest. More than likely the victim needed to seek revenge against the guy who did it to him.   Sometimes this can take years to boil over after festering for such a long time."

Roark objected, "Forgive me, if I may, but usually, isn't this a case of a priest molesting a young boy? The young boy, in this case, would have to be several years younger than the priest and the priest would have to be, I think, at least forty or so." Immediately, without a moment's hesitation, Roark thought about Pastor Gregory.

"Again, Inspector. I can only comment upon the mental state of someone who would do such a crime. You'll need to fill in the details yourself."

"Ignoring the suicide angle, you seem to be focused on only one other possibility. A pedophile type situation. Why no other theories?"

"As I said before, Inspector, the Bible says you may judge them by their acts. That's my belief and right now that's how I judge the Catholic Church."

"You seem to quote the Bible more than anything else."

"Yes, is there a problem, Inspector?"

"I just find it a little strange that a guy with your background would be using the Bible to test your theories and reach conclusions."

"There's nothing mutually inconsistent, Inspector, about examining human behavior by way of psychology, added with more than just a little help from the Bible. After all, the Bible is rich with truths about human nature. You could learn a lot from reading it, Inspector." Then he looked at Culpepper who seemed to be in a daze. "You, too," he said, waving a bony finger in Culpepper's direction.

"Well, we thank you for your time, Marvin," Roark said as he stood up to leave. "One more thing, Doctor."

"What's that, Inspector?"

"You got a nice family."

Schofield looked perplexed, not knowing what else to say. He wasn't sure if Roark's last statement was a compliment or sarcasm. So, he decided he had to get in the last word.

"Pedophiles, Inspector. They're practically all pedophiles. You find the one who's messing around with young boys and you'll find your answer."

Outside on the street, Culpepper asked Roark. "What do you think?"

"I think I need a drink."

CHAPTER TWENTY-TWO

"When's the last time you had a physical, inspector?"

She was tall, as tall as him. A soft face and soft eyes. He wasn't attracted to her in any way whatsoever but he had to admit she could very well be attractive to somebody. The thing that bothered him was the fact she was younger than he, he guessed, by five years or more and she was a she. Well, that's two things that bothered him. When it was mentioned to him that the first appointment that was available within the two-week deadline the Commissioner had given him, he had no choice. He tried to pretend it didn't matter. In any event, wearing a white smock over whatever else she was wearing underneath, she could have been a transvestite for all he knew. He'd just have to grin and bear it. Like he had a choice. He'd have to grin and bear it and get it over with.

"My last time? I think that's when I got out of the Navy."

"After World War II?" She joked.

"Christ, no. After Vietnam."

"I hope you didn't take offense, Inspector. It was a joke. Either way, that's a long time in between physicals."

"No offense taken. Wait. I forgot. I had one when I entered the police academy and I think I had another when I got out of the police academy."

"Not registering in your memory, Inspector?"

"Christ, all they do is stick a mirror in front of you to see if you fog it up and, if you do, you're fit for duty. That and stick their finger up your butt and you're on your way. Same with the Navy," Roark didn't believe a word of that story, exaggerating immensely, but it sounded good. He'd told it before.

"I see. Well, let's look at your chart. You had blood drawn a week ago?"

"Yes."

"Fasting for twelve hours?"

"Something like that."

"Well, let's see," she said with a mild show of irritation at his answer. Then she bobbed her head a couple of times and then squinted into the computer focusing on something or other.

"Hmmnnnnn..." She exhaled.

"Hmmnnnnn?" He repeated. "I'm not sure I like it when a doc, looking at my chart, says Hmmnnnnn."

"You have an elevated level of cholesterol, Inspector, along with high blood pressure.

Not a good combination for a man of your age. You're under fifty but it's not a good situation to be in at any age. What kind of diet are you on?"

"I'm on a seafood diet, Doc. I see food; I eat it."

"That's an old joke, Inspector."

"Sorry, I'll have to get some new material. Stand-up comedy is not my gig."

"Who cooks your meals?" She asked ignoring his last statement.

"You're looking at the cook."

"Just what I thought. And tell me I'm wrong. Everything you eat comes out of a bag, a box, or a can?"

"That's why they make can openers, doc."

"And eating five times a week at McDonalds is your view of fine dining?"

Roark was silent.

"Exercise? I know you're a cop but do you get daily exercise?"

"Being a cop means a lot of running around. Exercise? Whenever I get the urge I lay down until it goes away."

"Okay, Inspector. I'm putting you on pills. Morning and evening. We've got to get your cholesterol and blood pressure down to lower levels."

He'd never been sick a day in his life. Well, a cold every now and then. Doesn't everybody? The news hit him like a fifty-pound medicine ball in the gut. His dad died of a heart attack before he was sixty.

She mentioned the artery system being like plumbing, plumbing in your body and his plumbing was getting clogged up and, as she described it, when the plumbing gets real clogged up the pipes burst and people die. That was a horrible thought. Short of a bullet coming right at him this was as dangerous a situation as he could remember. Yet, no food out of a bag, a box, or a can? He'd starve to death.

"Does that do it, Doc? I'm a pill taker now?"

"One more thing, Inspector. I need for you to turn around and drop your trousers".

There's probably nothing more humiliating to a man than to be standing there with his pants and undershorts wrapped around his ankles, his bare butt out there to be seen in all its glory, butt hairs and all. But the thing about it that bothered Roark the most was that she treated it as though it was perfectly normal for a female to stick her finger up the butt of a male like there was nothing unusual about it, nothing to apologize for, nothing to be embarrassed about, nothing to even be shy about. Just business as usual. Finger up the butt.

He could hear her pulling plastic gloves on. He'd heard that sound before.

"Inspector Roark. You'll need to bend over and spread your cheeks. And, I recommend you turn your toes inward, pigeon-toed, if you will. It makes things a lot easier."

Pulling her hand out from the area in which it had been before, he heard her pull off the gloves and put them in a trash container. "You can get dressed now. We're done. I have to say, Inspector, you had a certain amount of dried fecal matter up there."

"What did you expect, Doc. Sugar?"

Chapter Twenty-Three

Next day he talked to Culpepper, "Hey, Roy boy, you work out in a gym, right? How much does that cost you to do that?"

"Sebastian. You thinking of working out? Hey, come with me to my club. I'll show you the ropes. I can get you in on a visitor's pass. No sweat."

"It's not for me, Roy boy. I just had somebody ask me about it, that's all. I didn't know what to tell him."

"Thirty bucks a month. That gym right around the corner. See you there, Sebastian. Friend of yours, my ass. It's you, isn't it?"

Roark found a gym across town, as far away from Culpepper's eyes as he could possibly get. Exercise, he thought to himself. This is the shits.

He made an appointment for a personal trainer realizing that he knew absolutely nothing about weights or any other piece of equipment in a gym and if there was one thing he would not allow it was a bunch of work-out nuts seeing him making a fool of himself. He waited in the lobby for his personal trainer to appear. Personal trainer.

Made it sound very special. Bobby Gates was the name of his appointment. Probably some super stud with arms as big as tree stumps. He'd never met a Bobby before. The only person that popped in his head with a name like Bobby was Bobby Bonds, the father of Barry Bonds. Bobby was a big Black man, as was his famous son. Oh, shit, he thought. Just what I fucking need.

"Are you, Mr. Roark?" She asked with the sweetest smile he'd ever seen this side of the Rocky Mountains.

He looked up to see a beautiful young girl who was as pregnant as a girl could be, "I'm waiting for Bobby what's his name."

"I'm Bobbie."

"How come you got a guy's name?"

"It's spelled B o b b i e, not B o b b y. It's short for Roberta. I never liked Roberta and I didn't want to go by Robin. That made me sound like a bird. So, I go by Bobbie. Are you ready to go, Mr. Roark?"

"Yeah, that's what I'm here for but are we going to be able to finish before you deliver or am I going to have to take you to the hospital?"

She patted her stomach proudly, "Oh, I'm still a month away. Please don't worry about my condition, Mr. Roark," she added. "I'm actually a very good athlete. When I'm not like this, I actually run triathlons. So, this is just a temporary condition."

"Not self-inflicted, I assume."

She smiled, "Ah, no. Not hardly."

"So," he asked, "what exactly is a triathlon?"

She smiled as proudly as she possibly could, "It's a long race, clear across town. First, we swim about a half mile, then we bike twelve miles, then we run 3 miles."

"Wouldn't it be easier to just take a bus?" He said dryly.

"Oh, Mr. Roark, I can see you're going to be a lot of fun to work with."

Good lord, thought Roark. Her belly looked bigger than any belly he'd ever seen. Good thing, he thought, that women do all the pregnancy and birth stuff. If men had to do it, the human race would have become extinct thousands of years ago.

"How long is this going to take?" He asked with some concern.

"You're scheduled for forty-five minutes, Mr. Roark. Is that too much?"

"No, I meant how long is going to take before my cholesterol is back to normal and I'm in better shape than I am now. I saw this movie once. It was John Travolta and he was dancer and before he made the movie somebody got him to work out and he changed from being a skinny kid to a guy who looked pretty good. Can't remember the movie?"

"Saturday Night Fever, maybe?"

"Yeah, I think so."

"So, you want to get built up to look like Travolta did in the movie?"

"Yeah, something like that."

"How many years has it been, Mr. Roark, since you did anything athletic?"

"I don't know. Maybe four or five years ago," he said with a plastic face, lying to his teeth.

"You want to look like John Travolta in the movie. I'd say we're looking at six months, depending upon how hard you want to work."

"Six months? I was hoping for six weeks."

So, they started out in the drills, Roark and his pregnant trainer. She worked him hard until he was out of breath and his shirt was heavy with dark sweat. Still, he never complained or asked to stop. If there ever was something you couldn't ever accuse Roark of being, it was a quitter. And, he was an impatient man that wanted results fast.

Chapter Twenty-Four

"Thank you for meeting me here, Kitty. The coffee house is too noisy and too many people, especially on a Saturday morning. Too many ears that might hear something."

"I like it here, in this park. It's so peaceful. I come here all the time," She said.

Roark paid her comment no mind, "Now, after you and Father Tim had dinner that night, when is the next time you talked to him?"

"Oh, gosh, it must have been a month. I think he was avoiding me. Because of what happened at the dinner. He told me, when he was driving me back to the library, it really scared him when that priest came over to our table. Oh, golly, you should have seen the look on his face."

"When you did meet, what did you talk about?"

She looked away.

"What?" Roark asked.

She didn't answer.

"Did he ever go to see your ex-husband?"

She then put her head down into her hands. Roark waited. It was a simple question, thought Roark.

"I'm sorry," she said, regaining her composure. "Yes, he did."

"And?"

"It didn't go well. Jerry got very belligerent and actually threatened Father Tim."

"That's it?"

"That was it. Jerry refused to cooperate and so Father Tim told me there wasn't much he could do. So, I asked again. This means I can never get married again and never have a baby?"

Roark felt a wave of frustration welling up inside him. That was one of the problems he had with the Catholic Church. They have all these rules, very strict rules which, in his estimation, are too strict. They ruin people's lives and explain it all away by suggesting it's God's will. How do they know it's God's will? How does anybody know that? It made him want to puke.

His mind wandered. What does life mean anyway? You get born, you go to school, you get a job, and you die. What's been accomplished? It was the same nagging thought that often preoccupied his mind, coming back to him again and again. The only thing that would make it go away short of turning to alcohol to ease his pain was to work. Digging deep into an investigation, he could forget about all these questions that had no answers.

What did it matter whether she was divorced or not divorced? Kitty had a right to a life, to do whatever, within reason, that she wanted to do.

So, he asked her, "Maybe you should just consider dropping the Church. Maybe join another church that allows for divorce and all the rest of it."

"I thought about that. More than once, I've thought about that but the Church has been my security blanket. I don't know what I would do without it. Join another church? I'd feel like a stranger."

Roark listened and figuratively scratched his head, trying to make any sense of what she had just said.

Interrupting his thoughts, she blurted it out.

"You know, Sebastian, you have beautiful hair."

"It's okay, I guess. That and a little bit of hair wax."

"You have an honest face. But you have sad eyes. That's what I noticed the first time we met."

"Kitty, can we get back to the subject. This is a criminal investigation."

"I'm sorry," She said. "I just wish we could talk about something other than murder. Really, I can't think of anything else to tell you."

Then they remained silent for a moment. Roark didn't know what to ask next or what to say. Then it just came out of his mouth.

"Someone left the cake out in the rain and I don't have the recipe to bake it anymore." He intoned a few words to break the silence.

"What did you just sing?"

"It was here, I think. Actually, I remember we were told that it was going to be happening, when I was a uniform on the force. I remember asking myself and anyone who would listen. 'Why the hell would they record it here? Of all places.'"

"What?"

"The song. You know, MacArthur Park. That British guy. What's his name? Harris, I think. They did the song here, when I was on the force."

"I hate to break the news to you. I don't think they recorded here. I'll bet they did it in a recording studio. But, whatever. I'm simply amazed. You're actually a romantic after all, Sebastian."

"I have my moments. Hey, look, we got to get back to business," he looked at her rather sternly. "Did you fall in love with Father Tim?"

"Oh my god, Sebastian, that's an awful question to ask."

"I have to ask. It's my job."

She hesitated, searching for words.

"Well?" he demanded.

"Of course I did. He was so handsome and he was kind."

"That's a terrible combination," mused Roark. "One I've never been accused of."

Then he asked the next question, "What about him? Did he? How shall I put this?"

"No, Inspector Roark. He didn't."

"Never touched you?"

"Never touched me. Not since, you know, that time I told you about when he hugged me and that innocent kiss on the cheek."

He couldn't help pushing the question. It was the one question that almost everyone would lie about. Why not her? Why not lie about it? He tried one more time, "You're sure about that?"

"Yes," she said defiantly. "I'm sure."

"Okay, I had to ask," he paused, thinking. There was another question but he was struggling to remember it. "Ah, I remember. This is a little off the subject but would you happen to know if Father Tim was left-handed or right-handed?"

"What a strange question, Sebastian. You never cease to amaze me."

"Well?"

"It was a funny thing. You know, one of those little things that people talk about. I think he dearly loved being a priest but nothing's perfect, I guess."

"Huh?" Sebastian was getting impatient.

"Giving out communion. Let me see if I can remember what he said. Oh, yeah. People, when they come to receive communion, expect the priest to put it on their tongue with his right hand. When it became necessary to make the sign of the cross, you know, Father, Son, and Holy Ghost, it's customary to do that with the right hand. So, he laughed. He said, you know I'm left-handed and I live in a right-handed world. He thought it was funny. Then, he told me something about being left-handed. Let me see if I can remember it. Maybe it'll help you."

"What did he say? I'm dying of curiosity."

"He said that there's a Latin word for left. 'Sinistro,' I think he said. And that's where we get our English word *sinister*."

"Huh? I don't get it."

"Well, he said, back in the old days, whenever somebody gave you something with their right hand that was a good thing. If they gave you something with their left hand, that was a bad thing. That's all I remember. Then he said something about left-handers being sinister. And...that's all I remember."

Roark slapped himself up side of the head.

"What?" She asked. "Why did you do that?"

"I forgot to take the chocolate chip cookies out of the oven."

"Huh?"

"Never mind. Now, let's talk about your ex-husband."

"Must we? Just thinking about him gives me the creeps. He was so mean."

"But you married the guy," Roark was again visited by those feelings of jealousy. Every time it was mentioned she was with someone else; those feelings would appear again. It upset him that they came and when they came, they wouldn't go away, no matter how hard he tried.

"Oh, he was charming when he wanted to be...when he wanted something. But he was very, I don't know, very unsure of himself. I think he was afraid I would leave him. He'd go into a rage whenever I wasn't home at the time he thought I should be home. Then we'd have sex and he'd be okay for a few days."

"I have to talk to him but I haven't been able to find his name anywhere. No Meadows in our records, not Jerry anyway."

"Oh, he's not Meadows. He's Jablonski."

"Huh?"

"I changed my name back to Meadows after the divorce."

"Okay. That helps. Jerry Jablonski."

"Actually, it's Jerome. Why do you need to talk to him?"

"Police business. I have to. He might shed some light on something. I'm not sure what."

"I wish you wouldn't."

"What?"

"He's an awful person and he's liable to tell you all sorts of things. About me. You can't believe anything he says."

"I'll keep that in mind. By the way, how big is this guy?"

"About your size. Maybe a little bigger. Why?"

"Doesn't matter. Hey, I got one last question. The guy you saw in church. Could it possibly have been your ex-husband?"

"Trust me. I would have known if it was him."

"He may have disguised himself. The church was kind of dark and you said you never got a good look at him and he kept turning away."

"Oh my god, Sebastian."

"What?"

"Just the thought of it, gives me the creeps."

The very next morning Roark decided to pay the coroner another visit. Being able to rule suicide out would be a step in the right direction. It was the way criminal investigations worked, through the process of elimination, narrowing it down until there is just one thing left. This was indeed a step in the right direction. All this time, he harbored a lingering thought that maybe, just maybe, the priest had done it himself and here he was, the great Detective Roark running all over town trying to find a murderer that didn't exist. Now that thought could be put to bed.

"Well," said the coroner. "It's you again. Did you forget something, Roark, or did you decide to take me up on that arm-wrestling contest?"

Roark got right to it, "I just learned that our dearly departed priest was left-handed."

"Really," the coroner seemed surprised. "And how did you come across that priceless bit of information?"

"It's not important how I got it. I'm just wondering."

"Yeah? Wondering what?"

"Why you didn't talk to me about that when I was first down here. It would have helped a lot."

"Roark," she stammered. "Look around you. What do you see? A room full of stiffs, all dead, some of them involuntarily. All of them, commanding my attention. And you're asking me whether I knew one of them was left-handed."

"Well, it's a simple question."

The coroner folded her arms over her chest in a stance fluctuating between anger and self-doubt. "I suppose," she resigned. "If I felt it was suicide, I would have checked to see if his left hand or his right hand was more developed. But, that's not always the case. Besides, he could have been ambidextrous."

"I have it on good authority he was left-handed."

"Then I think I agree, Roark, it doesn't look like suicide, if what you say is true."

"Good. I just wanted to hear it from you."

"Well, now you have it. Any more questions, while you're here?"

Roark stood motionless, an empty look on his face.

"So, now you have your answer. By the way, why couldn't you have just called me? You know, the telephone; that thing someone invented a hundred years ago?"

"Oh, yeah. That thing. I like the personal touch."

Chapter Twenty-Five

Despite her objection and the pleading look in her face, he was determined to talk to Kitty's ex-husband. He might very well have absolutely nothing to do with Father Tim's death but, then again, he might have everything to do with it. Only time would tell. And time was still ticking.

Funny thing about a murder investigation. It's in the news media that day and the next. Maybe for an entire week, it's on everybody's mind. Then, after a week, it's not mentioned so much. The Commissioner had told him, no, *threatened* him, that he'd better solve this in a hurry or the Archdiocese of Los Angeles would reign down upon her with all the power they might possess. Now, it seemed that threat had been put on the back burner. No longer was there a media blitz searching for answers. It's almost as though, except for the immediate family of the deceased and perhaps the immediate family of the murderer, it's yesterday's news, soon to be forgotten, possibly forever. Isn't that the way it always is, Roark asked himself. And, if it wasn't for bulldog detectives like himself a number of these murders would not only be forgotten but they would also go unsolved. Not on his watch, he assured himself.

Culpepper? His partner? Where was he now? Apparently, he got reassigned to a new case. Probably investigating who put some old lady's cat up in a tree, thought Roark. It was the best news he'd heard for awhile. No partner to hang on his coattails.

It really bothered him that Kitty very clearly did not want him talking to her ex-husband. Why? What did she say? He might say things about her. Duh? What ex-husband isn't going to say bad things about the ex-wife? It's the nature of things. Anyway, what could he possibly say about her? What could he say that Roark would even begin to believe? The guy was obviously a jerk. Jerry the Jerk, that's what Roark decided to call him.

He was starting to hate the guy already, never having met him. How could he mistreat a beautiful young woman like Kitty? It's not uncommon in his line of work for that to be the case, but Roark still found it detestable that a man would physically abuse a woman. What kind of a man does that?

The other thing that bothered him was the fact she made it clear that her ex-husband, now Jerry the Jerk, had probably moved. No, wait. She said he had moved. How would she know that unless...unless what? He couldn't think of a reason. One thing for sure, if she didn't want him to find her ex-husband why did she volunteer to give Roark his real name? Maybe she wasn't thinking. In Roark's experience women didn't always think the way he thought they should. For sure, they didn't think the way he did and that fact, and that fact alone, was the reason he knew he'd never understand women.

She probably thought he'd never find him with just a name. Los Angeles is a big city but Roark had his ways. If the guy drove a car, he'd find him. According to the Department of Motor Vehicles there were two listings for J. Jablonski. What the fuck, thought Roark. What were the chances of two people with the same name living in Los Angeles? The first name he checked out had a first name of Jessica. That narrowed his list down to one, an apartment in the cheap section of Santa Monica.

As he approached what looked like every other cheap two-story apartment building, he gathered his thoughts. As was always the case, he had his service revolver strapped inside his light jacket. Just in case the guy got hostile. Then he remembered he didn't shoot before when he should have, back then, when he was a patrolan. Would he be able to now? Actually, he preferred to beat the guy's brains out, if he could.

After just a couple of weeks, he felt stronger, lifting those weights in the gym on an accelerated schedule. Then she had him jumping rope. Pushing sleds across a rug. Working with a heavy medicine ball. She was a virtual task master and he began to love it. He began to love seeing her, in a strange, inexplicable way. Although ten to fifteen years his junior he thought he could easily fall in love with her given the chance. Just two obstacles at the moment. She was very pregnant and probably much in love with some other lucky guy. In any event, with his new body and newly found strength and agility, he was convinced he could handle Jablonski. At least that's what he hoped.

Jablonski? The guy may be a jerk, thought Roark, but he had few good years making love to Kitty Meadows. That, in itself, made him a lucky man and Sebastian Roark an envious man. Damn. One more reason to beat his brains out, shoot him or all of the above.

He knocked on the door. Nobody answered. He knocked again. Nobody answered. He had purposely selected a Saturday morning for a surprise visit thinking that someone would be home. No answer. No point in leaving a message so he headed back down the stairs.

Halfway down an irritated voice called out to him, "Who are you?"

Roark stopped in his tracks and pulled out his identification, "Detective Sebastian Roark. I have a few questions I'd like to ask you."

The man in the doorway froze, holding the door slightly open while Roark climbed the stairs and looked at him eyeball to eyeball. The man had obviously just gotten out of bed, no doubt sleeping off a hangover if his sloppy appearance was any indication. His hair was disheveled, hanging haphazardly over his forehead. The man squinted through the narrow opening, looking at Roark's identification which Roark practically stuck in his face. The man opened the door and slowly retreated. Roark took this as an invitation to enter.

Once inside the room, Roark looked around. Typical low rent one-bedroom apartment with a cheap and dirty couch, a simulated wood coffee table upon which there were two empty beer cans. The obligatory TV sitting on a chrome stand. A lamp on a lamp table, the only other furniture in the room. The man slumped onto the soft couch and rubbed his eyes.

Roark looked around for a place to sit. The couch wasn't that appealing. He grabbed a wooden, poorly painted, white kitchen table chair and brought it into the living room, all the while keeping his eyes on Jablonski, his revolver at the ready.

"I'll sit here," Roark declared as he reversed the chair and sat on it backwards facing the couch. "You Jerry Jablonski?"

"Yeah," he mumbled. "That's me."

"You look like you had a bad night?" Roark suggested without a touch of sympathy, more of an accusation than anything else.

"Yeah, man. It was a bad night. But it wasn't my fault. The stupid asshole was jogging at midnight. How the hell would I know? I never saw him."

"What are you talking about?"

"Last night. I admit it, I hit the guy. But he was okay. Cursing and swearing at me. He gave me the finger and ran off. I guess he wasn't too hurt."

Roark rubbed his chin. Wasn't expecting this, "Look, I'm not here to ask you about last night but, while we're on the subject, were you drunk?"

"Yeah, man. Drunk as a skunk. I admit it," he started to say something else and then he clammed up. "You gonna make a federal case out of it?"

Roark had to think this through. The guy had just admitted driving drunk and hitting a pedestrian. A guy running. Didn't matter. It's battery or assault; one of those. Then came the question, should he arrest the guy for a self-admitted crime, haul his sorry ass downtown and grill him under the lights? One problem. Miranda.

Fucking Miranda. It's handcuffed the police for decades now. Worse than that; it's set free more criminals than anyone really knows. You have the fucking right to remain silent and I can't do a fucking thing about it. You have the right to an attorney and, if you can't afford one, the taxpayers will furnish you with an attorney. So, I warn your sorry ass, don't say a thing because it can be used in court against you until some smartass lawyer can think of some technicality to get you off. Some kind of justice system we have in this country, thought Roark, sadly.

As a policeman, he'd read up on Miranda. What the hell was that all about? Who the hell was Miranda? What he found out was Miranda was a bad guy. He got off from the crime he committed in the particular instance that gave rise to the so-called Miranda decision but he wound up in jail anyway for another crime, at least that's what Roark remembered from his reading. Then there was the good part. Roark wasn't sure if his memory was correct or not but that is what he remembered. Apparently, Miranda, either after he got out of jail or while he was still in there, got killed. The only important thing, as far as Roark was concerned, was he got what he deserved. And here's the best part of all, remembered Roark. The guy who killed Miranda got off because the police had failed to advise the perp of his newly adjudicated Miranda rights. How fucking ironic is that? He wasn't absolutely sure he remembered all that correctly but it didn't matter. That's the story he told anybody who was interested in listening, and it made for a good story.

One good thing about Miranda that he was sure of, unless he arrested Jablonski there was no need to advise him of his Miranda rights. Besides, if he hauled him downtown and booked him on the charge of drunk driving and battery, some lawyer would have him out in five minutes. There was no proof and Jablonski would probably deny everything. Besides, that's not the reason for his visit. He had bigger fish to fry.

Roark answered the man's question, "No, I'm interested in something else. Information, that's all. But I would suggest that you don't drive drunk in the future." That last bit of advice was intended to put the man at ease. It was always best to put witnesses at ease even if he expected they were a lying sack of shit, such as he suspected Jablonski was going to be.

"I lost my job. What's a guy supposed to do?"

"Get another job, I suppose," Roark retorted. Noticing the porn magazines with half naked women on the covers as they lay strewn across the coffee table, Roark said with as much sarcasm as he could muster,

"Maybe you'll have to cut back on buying porn magazines."

Jablonski made no attempt to hide them, actually showing no emotion at all, as if Roark had been referring to the Wall Street Journal.

Roark continued, "Hey look, I'm here to ask you about Kitty Meadows."

Jerry fell back onto the couch whereas before, he had been sitting slumped forward with his elbows on his knees and his head in his hands. Now slumped on the couch staring up at the ceiling he exhaled. "Kitty Meadows? You mean Kitty Jablonski, my wife?"

"I hear she's your ex-wife and she changed her name back to Meadows," As soon as he said it, Roark regretted it. There was no reason to divulge information to Jablonski. He hoped he'd soon forget it, considering he was hung over.

"What do you want to know about her? Up to her old tricks?"

Roark was always tempted, when asking an unsuspecting witness for vital information, to not tell the witness why he was asking that particular question. Unfortunately, that's not the exact protocol he'd been taught. Those learned and pious folks that made the rules made it a rule that it's best to inform the witness why he or she was being asked certain questions. Without that knowledge they would have no reason to judge the seriousness of the questions and might indicate, if challenged later, that they answered in an incorrect way because they had no idea what it was about. Be it correct or not, Roark was not shy about keeping things as secretive as he wanted them to be and sharing information with witnesses only to the extent he felt they needed to know.

He wanted to see Jablonski's reaction. "It's a murder case."

"You're shitting me?" Jablonski said with genuine surprise. Either that or he was an accomplished actor, thought Roark.

"Who did she murder?"

"A Catholic priest," Roark answered continuing in the vein of trying to shock Jerry the Jerk into betraying something. So far nothing was working.

"You got to be kidding me. A priest? Don't tell me, it's that guy who came poking around here asking me if I'd testify that we never really were married so she could get an annulment and run off with some other sucker. I told him to get the fuck out of my house. Is that the guy?"

Roark ignored his question, "So, he came to see you? And that's all you two talked about? His request and your refusal and your polite request that he leave your house?" Roark relished in his sudden sarcastic wit. Jablonski deserved it.

"Yeah. That's it. What else did you think we'd be talking about? I got nothing to say to no priest or the Catholic Church. And helping her? Don't make me laugh."

"Okay, tough guy. You hate her, you hate the Catholic Church. What else do you hate?"

Jerry remained silent as though he hadn't heard the question. Then off the back of the coach he leaned forward in a prayer-like stance, his elbows on his thighs and his hands together, as if he was going to pray.

"I was actually going to be a priest. I'm sure you don't believe that but it's true. You can look it up."

"What? You get a varsity jacket if you once studied to be a priest?" Oh, shit, thought Roark. Here I am trying to get away from the Catholic Church and Catholics and they seem to be popping up all over the place, faster than ants at an Iowa picnic. Must be some kind of conspiracy, something intending to drive him nuts. "I will look it up. So, what happened?"

"What do you mean?"

"I mean you said you studied to be a priest. If this is how studying for the priesthood winds up, I can see why they are running out of priests these days."

Jerry ignored Roark's tirade, now becoming more relaxed and accustomed to his modus operandi.

"It was her that caused me to quit. I wish I'd never met her. She's a..."

"Just stick to the facts, okay?"

"It was after my first year in the seminary. I went home for the summer. I got a job. A lifeguard at a public pool. I thought that would be perfect. Outside, sitting in a chair just watching people swim. What could be easier than that?"

"Can you cut through the shit and get to the bottom line?"

"She was there. Every day. She'd show up for some reason. Looking all sexy in a bikini. She always had something to ask me. Whenever my shift was over, she'd be right there asking where I went to school and what was I thinking about for a career and stuff like that."

"You told her to get lost because you were studying to be a priest and you weren't the least bit tempted by some sexy babe in a bikini, right?"

"I told her I was going to UCLA and studying to be a doctor."

"You lied to her."

"Only partly, the part about UCLA. I didn't want her to know I was studying to be a priest. I was afraid she'd think I was some kind of a freak or a queer. So, I lied."

"The part about studying to be a doctor? That wasn't a lie."

"No. Being a priest is a doctorate in religion. So that part was, technically, true."

"Bullshit. You got the girl's hopes up."

Jerry shook his head as if to deny Roark's accusation, "It wasn't like that. She's the one who started it. She said she didn't know how to swim and asked if I'd give her lessons. I figured, what can it hurt? So, I went to her apartment where there was a pool. The next thing I know she's loses the top to her bathing suit and we're arm in arm, standing in water up to our shoulders. Sooner than I could stop her she had her hand inside my swimming trunks. I was paralyzed. She smiled at me and seemed to enjoy the moment. I never felt anything in my life as good as that. We went up to her apartment and we had sex. I couldn't help myself. I knew it was wrong," he shook his head again as if to erase the memory. "I just couldn't help myself."

"I'm still waiting for the bottom line."

"I was getting ready to go back to the seminary and before I could think of some story, like I was moving back east or something like that, she said she was pregnant. I actually had my bags packed and now I've got a pregnant girl on my hands who insisted we get married. I didn't have much choice. I enrolled in classes at UCLA. The priesthood was gone."

"You could have gotten an abortion."

"That's not possible. She was Catholic; I thought I was Catholic. I didn't really know any more what I was."

"So, then what happened?"

"We did it right. We got married in the church and waited for the baby to come." Jablonski made faces, peculiar faces, like he was being tortured internally by the past. "Three months after we were married, she lost the baby. She blamed me."

"Blamed you. Why would she blame you?"

"She said she lost the baby because she had to work all day on her feet to support us while all I did was sit around in class at UCLA. So here I was. An upset wife, no baby, no job. The priesthood a thing of the past. I couldn't help it. I just didn't know what to do."

"Yeah?"

"I started drinking but that didn't help things."

"It seldom does."

"Things went to hell after that."

"You started to abuse her?"

"Huh? Never. I would never abuse her or anyone else for that matter."

"She said you did."

"She's a liar. It was all her doing."

"What?"

"The kinky sex. It started out she wasn't satisfied with normal sex. She had to have it different ways, on her stomach, doggy style. Every different position she could think of. I was kind of shocked but I went along with it. Then she got into more stuff.

Ice cubes and syrup that she told me to lick off her body. I did it to please her."

Roark was entranced. Never in his professional career had he heard what he considered to be a pack of lies but a pack of lies told so convincingly. He almost started to feel sorry for Jablonski, the ex-seminarian who just couldn't help himself to avoid the clutches of a supposed wicked woman. Then he snapped out of it.

"I think you're lying."

"I figured that. I know. You look at me and I'm a mess. Hung over. I live in a cheap apartment, thanks to her. You know she even made a charge against me that I was a sexual predator and now that's on my record. Try getting a job with that on your record. You can believe whatever you want, Detective Roark. Don't matter to me. I'm done with her. I'm done with the Catholic Church. I'm done with...a lot of things."

Roark felt like asking. Done with a lot of things to the extent you'd commit murder? But didn't. Later on, he wished he had.

So, he settled for one last, more simple question, "You got any knives, Jablonski?"

"Knives? Why? You want to slash your wrists, Roark?"

"No, shithead, I'm asking if you got any knives. I'd like an answer."

"The only knives I have are in the kitchen. Help yourself."

CHAPTER TWENTY-SIX

Roark came away from Jablonski's place with mixed emotions. He was either a prolific liar or the most maligned person in the history of the world. Problem for Roark was to decide which it was. Liar or pitiful soul? It wasn't that hard for Roark to reach an initial decision. For the last decade or so he had been engaged in a job function that motivated just about everyone he talked to into being a liar. Even witnesses sometimes lie. Why? To make themselves feel more important. To protect the fact that maybe they were some place where they shouldn't be. Not wanting to be involved. Fearful they might have to go to trial and get up on the witness stand. Any number of reasons. Criminals lie like fleas on a dog. It's a total surprise if anything that comes out of their mouth proves to be true. Believing Jerry the Jerk, meant he'd have to then begin to treat Kitty Meadows as a horrible person and he didn't want to have to do that. So, it was a lot easier to assume Jerry the Jerk lied about everything.

He called Culpepper, "Hey, Roy boy, you got some free time."

"What do you want, Sebastian? Go out for a drink?"

"No, I want you to follow a person of interest for awhile."

"How long is awhile?"

"A week, maybe more. Remember, technically speaking, you're still assigned to this case."

"It's gonna cost you, Roark. You turn over to me that blonde you've been hustling. Okay? I'll keep an eye on her and your person of interest."

"See this is why I call you jackass, Culpepper. You don't treat this job as a serious job, as a professional. I need your help, god dammit, and you pull this shit on me."

Culpepper agreed to keep an eye on Jablonski. Roark suggested they go right away so he could show him where Jablonski lived.

Culpepper said he had to get changed because he'd be following Roark on his motorbike.

"Changed? You need to get changed to ride a motorbike?"

"Can't ride in this outfit, Roark. It would look dorky. "

Roark impatiently waited for Culpepper to appear. Out came a figure he didn't recognize. It was Culpepper all decked out in a spandex body suit carrying a huge helmet that looked every bit the size of an orange crate.

"What the fuck is this, Culpepper? You look like you're going into space."

"My motorbike riding outfit. What's wrong, Sebastian. You never rode a bike? Besides, this'll be a better disguise to follow your guy. I wear my street clothes and he's going to spot me before I get off the bike."

Space helmet and spandex body suit? Didn't much matter to Roark. Two things got accomplished. One, he gets Culpepper out of his hair and, two, he had somebody watching Jablonski.

Culpepper got on his bike, positioned his helmet, and, with all the precautionary protocol of a jet pilot he checked all his gauges. Roark watched with amazement and a certain amount of contempt. Before heading to his car, he said, with his hand cupped over his mouth for that special effect: "Ah, Houston this is control tower. Prepare for takeoff. Roy Culpepper is going into space."

That night, Roark went to bed tired but, as usual, couldn't get to sleep. Two or three glasses of wine or beer was his limit but tonight he'd emptied an entire bottle of cheap wine. Laying there, tossing back and forth, he played it over and over in his mind. Just for the moment, he thought, I'll focus on Kitty. Could she have done it? And why? He put himself in her shoes and tried as best he could to think of her doing it and how she might have planned it.

At first, Roark really struggled with the alternative to Jablonski being a liar. But then it wouldn't be the first time in the history of the world that a woman used sex to destroy a man. Take Sampson and Delilah. Look at what she did to him. He loved that movie. Hedy Lamarr as the seductive wench. Victor Mature as Sampson. He was perfect. A big man with a menacing face but he was no match for Hedy Lamarr, the ultimate seductive wicked woman. She went traveling in a caravan in a territory where Sampson was known to be moving about as he continued his private war with the Philistines. She dismissed her guards knowing that, as vulnerable a position as that would put her in, she knew that Sampson couldn't resist taking possession of her. She plied him with wine and sex and he fell for her charms. Roark was always fascinated by the scene where she offered him the first cup of wine. She had put a sleeping potion in one of the glasses and offered a clean glass of wine to Sampson leaving the cup with the sleeping potion in her hand as if she was going to drink it. But Sampson, though he loved and coveted her, still didn't trust her so he took the cup with the sleeping potion out of her hand and gave her the cup she had offered to him. She outsmarted him. And poor, unsuspecting Sampson was soon fast asleep. She then gave him the most famous haircut of all time.

Was Kitty Meadows his Delilah and he Sampson? Soon, he was fast asleep.

169

CHAPTER TWENTY-SEVEN

Kitty Meadows calculated her every move. Saturday night confession. It was the perfect time. She would confront Father Tim. In the confessional, there was no way he could escape or get upset. He'd have to listen to her and face the situation once and for all instead of the evasive tactics he had used so far.

They had made love and that was a fact. The reasons might be in dispute but what wasn't in dispute was the fact that they had made mad, passionate love. As a result, he now belonged to her and there was no way around that, no matter what he said.

If that wasn't enough to get him to abandon the priesthood and bind him to her then how about that tidy little issue of her being pregnant with his child? It worked before and it can work again, she thought.

Sure, he was a priest but that could be changed. Nothing is permanent. Anything can be changed if you want it to be changed and she was banking on him making the decisions that needed to be made. If not, then he'd pay. And pay dearly.

Yes, she would confront him, in the confessional. What better place to tell him exactly what was on her mind? A life with Father Tim. No. Wait. No more Father Tim. From now on, it would be her and Tim Hanrahan, as handsome a man as she had ever seen. He was now hers. No way around it. He was hers.

When he turned her down, Kitty Meadows was heartbroken, betrayed beyond her wildest dreams because she had convinced herself that he would agree and make the promises to her she desperately wanted to hear. This was now the third time a man had broken her heart, had broken every promise she thought he had made to her.

If three men could treat her like dirt and break their promises, why not four or five? How many more times would it happen to her? That very strong possibility is what infuriated her the most. She got so mad she lost control.

Instead of leaving the church after her failed attempt in the confessional, she sat for a moment, not far away, in one of the pews. She was powerless to move, engulfed in grief and disappointment. Wearing her usual running outfit, she turned the back pack around to her stomach. Inside the pack was a knife, the knife she always carried when jogging or going to confession. A girl just never knows when some man bent on ravaging her body would leap out at her and the knife would be her only defense.

It was one of the few things that she got out of the marriage to Jerry Jablonski, that and the small figurine statue of the Blessed Virgin. To be sure, the former was more practical than the latter. The former had guarded her against any number of nasty men who have might leaped out of the bushes as she ran by on one of her jogs.

Father Tim had to pay. She looked around and there was nobody in the church. Nobody. Just her and Father Tim. He had the light off in his little section of the confessional. It would be easy. The element of surprise was on her side. He'd never seduce a woman again.

Roark woke up in the middle of the night. Even with the window open in his bedroom and the cool evening breeze blowing in he was bathed in sweat. At first, he had no clue where he was.

He looked at the clock radio on his night stand. As it usually did, it was blinking 12:00, 12:00, blinking and blinking and blinking. He vowed to fix that but right now he needed to figure out what was going on in his head, which was pounding.

Was it a dream? Or not? Kitty was there. And the knife. And everything was so vivid. He got up and looked at his watch. 3:00 in the morning. Too early to get up, too late to go back to sleep. His head pounding, he took a couple of aspirin with a glass of cold milk and tried to go back to sleep. A whole bottle of wine. No wonder.

Kitty? Did she really do it? Sweet lovable Kitty? Was she the monster Jerry the Jerk portrayed her to be or was his mind so twisted in knots that he couldn't think straight anymore?

CHAPTER TWENTY-EIGHT

That dream had just been too real. It had details that he couldn't have made up had he wanted to. But then, he had to admit; it was a dream. Still, it couldn't be dismissed as if it had no possible reality. He had to know and had to know right now whether it could possibly have happened the way he dreamed it. Previously, they had met in the police station, a local coffee shop, and then a city park. It was now time to meet where she lived. That way he hoped to understand her a lot better, seeing where she lived, what things might be laying about, anything that might tell him what she was really all about. The very next night, when he knew she was home he knocked on her door.

"Sebastian, what on earth are you doing here?" Bare-footed, she wore a pair of old jeans and a pullover T-shirt. He could tell she was braless. The T-shirt was stretched to the limits. She immediately put her arms across her chest. "I wasn't expecting you," she said, very much annoyed.

"May I come in?" After some hesitation she allowed it to happen by backing away from the door and shrugging her shoulders.

"I was in the neighborhood and I thought I'd just drop in on you and see how you were doing."

"You mean you've come to question me some more about Father Tim?" As she said it, she had released her arms away from her chest and then quickly folded them back remembering they covered that which she didn't want Roark to see.

"Kitty," he said softly, almost affectionately. "I've got to solve this murder. Don't you understand? And, like it or not, you're the one person, if not the only person, who can help me."

"Very well," she conceded. "I'm sorry. I'm just a bit jumpy because every time we talk there seems to be some suggestion coming out of your mouth that somehow Father Tim and I were romantically involved."

"May I sit?" She pointed to an upholstered straight chair on the opposite side of the coffee table that now separated them. Strewn on the table were the usual magazines a young woman would have. Nothing at all revealing. She positioned herself on the couch, her arms remaining folded over her chest.

"I talked to your ex-husband, by the way. He sends his regards."

No reaction was forthcoming. She just realigned her lips and jaw as if she had bit onto something that didn't taste very good.

She then replied with a distant amount of interest, "So what did you think of him?"

"Charming fellow. Very revealing."

"You're kidding. Are you sure you got the right Jerry Jablonski?"

"Yes, I'm sure. He seemed to know all about you. How many guys named Jerry Jablonski do you know?"

She ignored his question, looking down at her arms crossed over her chest, "I suppose I should put something else on. I wasn't expecting company."

"You answered the door."

She ran into the bedroom while Roark sat there wondering. Would she come roaring out of the bedroom like a witch on a broomstick, wielding a knife, the matching knife to the one she used to murder Father Tim. Or maybe a gun? He shifted in his seat so he could disengage the holster to the service revolver that was fastened to the back of his belt. If she did come out in attack mode, could he shoot her? He hoped he wouldn't have to find out.

Once again, to his painful disappointment, he was reminded of that time on the force when he had failed to pull the trigger and his partner almost got killed.

She came out with a different top on and had added a bra underneath it, "There. Is that better?" she said, flopping back onto the couch.

He smiled and then relaxed his hand off the holster of his revolver, twisting around so that she might not notice at all what he was doing.

"Okay, let's talk about Jablonski," Roark now had to lie, lie through his teeth, but he felt it justified. "He said you took two things from him." He let the question linger, looking for a reaction. She showed some concern but not enough to reveal anything specific. "Besides the statue he says you took a knife. A knife that belonged to him."

"I told you already, Sebastian. She gave the statue to me."

"He says she gave it to both of you as a wedding gift."

She remained silent, as if she had no answer.

Roark pressed on, "What about the knife?"

"Tell me, Sebastian, you didn't come to see me to find out if I took one of his knives? Is that really a big deal?"

"Could be, if it turns out it was the murder weapon."

She frowned and went into an intense internal struggle. Roark judged it to be she was forming a story, an outright lie that would disconnect her from the knife.

Finally, she gave her answer, "There were never any knives as far as I know," She paused, then continued. "He does have a gun, though. He showed it to me once and that's the only time I ever saw it. I don't know where he kept it and we never talked about it again. I think he hid it because he knew someday, the way he was treating me, I might pull it out and shoot him."

"You were tempted?"

She rolled her eyes, "Guns scare me. I don't want to be anywhere near them."

"How about the knife?"

"I told you. If he had a knife, I never saw it."

Roark decided to let that rest. Then he changed tactics.

"He says you were into kinky sex."

She stiffened as if struck by an electric shock. She wrapped her arms around her chest once more, in an act of complete self-defense, "I did those things to please him. They were his idea. I went along with it because ... well..."

"Yeah? Because?"

"I was afraid of him. I just did what he wanted me to do. If I didn't, he'd make me pay one way or another. You just don't seem to understand. You're a man so I guess I shouldn't expect you to."

"Try me."

She burst into tears, her head in her hands. Then she looked at him with the most pitiful look he'd ever seen on the face of a young woman, "It was always the same. If I did something he didn't like, he would punish me. Sometimes it was just cursing at me. Other times it was worse. But if I did something he liked, he would reward me. He'd bring home perfume or flowers and tell me sweet things, nice things a girl likes to hear. I was like a dog. That's how he treated me. Reward and punishment. It never stopped."

Roark sat rigid. Thinking. Wondering. She noticed his body language and it wasn't good.

"You don't believe me, do you? You think I'm the kind of a person who would do those things. You probably think I killed Father Tim. I thought we..." Then her voice trailed off, in mid-thought.

He couldn't think of anything else to say or ask, "I don't know what to believe."

"Please go," she whispered in a hoarse voice. "I can't bear another minute of this."

Chapter Twenty-Nine

Roark quizzed Culpepper, "Tell me. What've you got?"

"It's gonna cost you, Roark. A drink. Maybe two and I'll spill my guts."

They agreed to meet in a sports bar. The waitress had a low-cut top on that revealed more cleavage than was proper even in a dumpy bar like the one they were in. Culpepper was his usual self—a complete ass. First words out of his mouth were, "I'll have two of those," The girl faked a frown, pretending to be insulted but really wasn't. Culpepper saw Roark's disapproving look and clarified his order. "A vodka martini, shaken, not stirred. Like that guy in the movies."

The girl rolled her eyes as if to say she'd heard them all, all the dumb things that guys in bars say to waitresses. She looked at Roark, fearing the worst.

"I'll have a beer, one of those foreign brands."

"Which one?"

"Surprise me, will you?"

She skirted off with Culpepper following every step she took until she was out of his view. "Some dish, right?"

"What have you got, Roy?"

"The guy's a jerk but he's predictable. A predictable jerk."

"Explain."

"Every night, he goes to the same bar. Gets plastered. Staggers back to his apartment and then, pretty soon, it's lights out."

"He told me he got fired. Has he got a new job yet?"

"Not that I can see. Hey, but I can't watch him 24/7 either. So maybe he goes out somewhere. To a job maybe."

"That's okay, Roy. I just want to make sure he's still there and not planning to move to Alaska."

"Yeah. Well, he's there all right. But tell me, Roark, what are you looking for? What should I be looking for?"

"I wish I knew," Roark said wistfully. "Actually, I have an idea. I think he's very possibly our perp but I don't know why and I don't have a shred of evidence tying him to the crime. And, when I talk to him, he gets very belligerent. I guess that's to be expected. I just think..." Then he paused. "I think I'd like to put him off guard. Catch him, by surprise. Make it look like it was totally unplanned. You know. Bump into the guy by accident. But a bar is too noisy and not very professional."

"I don't get it, Roark. What's the big deal? Just take him down to the station."

"No, that wouldn't work. I need to somehow win his confidence. Make him believe I've just about got all I need to pin the murder on Kitty. That sort of thing. He hates her enough he might just spill his guts and, in so doing, say something I can use."

"Geez, Roark. That's fucking brilliant. Gotta hand it to you. I would never have thought of that."

Roark dismissed his compliment with a wave of his hand. Culpepper, he thought to himself. Why me, Lord?

"How about a porn shop?"

"What?"

"Yeah, twice a week, he goes into this same movie rental. They got this back area. You know, where they keep the porno stuff. He picks something out, returns it in a couple of days, then checks out a new one."

"That's interesting bit it makes things a little complicated as far an accidental meeting."

"No sweat, Roark. It's like clockwork. Monday night around six o'clock, sure as shit, he goes there first, then hits the bar around the corner. Same thing on Thursday. Six o'clock. Never fails. At least the two weeks I've been watching him."

Roark seriously wondered if this plan was going to work. What if Jablonski never showed? How would Roark feel waiting around in a sleazy area of a movie rental place? He'd wasted enough time as it was. But it was worth a try. He didn't have any other ideas worth pursing at the moment.

He'd pretend to Jablonski that he had the goods on Kitty. That's what troubled him. Could he fake it and pull it off? Aside from that awful dream he had a couple of nights ago, he really had nothing tangible to pin on her. And, there was one thing that really troubled him to the point of eliminating her from his list of prospects.

If, by chance, she did it. Why on earth would she have volunteered out of the clear blue sky to come to the police station and admit she was there? Why, indeed? She would never have been picked out as a witness. It made no sense. It made no sense at all and, making no sense, it brought him to one conclusion. She had no part in it. He was happy with that conclusion, dream or no dream.

CHAPTER THIRTY

Roark stationed himself in an obscure spot in the movie rental and waited. A little after six o'clock, sure enough, Jablonski comes into the rental, returns a movie into the return basket and heads for the adult area. Roark waits a few moments then follows him in there.

"Well, well. Fancy meeting you here, Jablonski. I see you're trying to educate yourself with the right kind of movies. Nice try."

"You following me, Detective?"

"No, we just happen to use the same movie rental."

"Bullshit."

Roark ignored his comment and whispered, "Look I'm not here to shake your shit. Actually, I need your help. Let's you and I take a little walk."

"Why should I take a fucking walk with you? You gonna arrest me for renting a movie?"

Roark gently put his hand on Jablonski's arm in a manner intended to calm him down. Then he whispered in his ear, "I think I've got her, Jerry. I just need a little help from you, then I'm going to arrest her."

Outside they started walking towards the ocean, just a couple of blocks away. The summer heat was gone, replaced by cool breezes coming off the water. They passed more old run-down apartment buildings, like the one Jablonski lived in and post World War II houses with little front yards and burnt grass. Most everybody was inside, watching TV. As they neared the beach things got noisier and then a lot noisier and a lot more crowded.

"Where we going, Roark? You know this is cutting into my drinking time."

"It's better for your liver."

"What do you want? This wasn't a chance meeting."

They crossed famed Ocean Avenue which ran along the beach, separating the bars and tourist shops on one side from the beach goers and the joggers and skaters on the other. On the inland side there were more bars than a person could count, tattoo places, shops selling cheap swimming and snorkeling attire, and other assorted stores appealing mostly to young people with too much time on their hands and too much cash in their pockets. Or was it too much plastic in their wallets? On the ocean side was a paving made for skating, skateboarding, running and walking. It would have been easy to get hit by either a jogger or an errant skate board.

Palm trees punctuated the walkways. Firmly planted every few feet it seemed, they stood silently in the gentle breeze. Then came the sand. Now after six o'clock, and there was still a lot of action on the beach. Summer time in Santa Monica. It never ends, until dark, that is.

"Let's walk out on the beach."

"Huh?"

"C'mon, Jerry, take your shoes off and roll up the cuffs of your pants."

They weaved their way through the people who were still lounging on the sand or lounging on their blankets, hanging on to the last bit of sunlight, waiting for the sun to set over the ocean right in front of them, with a priceless, unobstructed view.

At the water's edge Roark and Jablonski stopped. To their right was famed Santa Monica pier. To the left, nothing but miles of beach as far as the eye could see.

"Let's walk."

"What kind of weird interrogation technique have you got going here, Roark?"

"I just want to have a little chat. You worried about something?"

Joggers went past them in the opposite direction, sometimes coming upon them from the rear, passing them as they breathed heavily.

"I talked to your ex. She gave me a slightly different slant on your relationship than you gave me a couple of weeks ago."

"I'm not surprised. Tell me, Roark, you didn't fall for her bullshit?"

"Jerry, she says she saw you at the church that night," Roark lied.

"Oh yeah? What night would that be, Roark?"

"You know goddamn well what night that would be. Stop jerking my chain, Jerry, or I'll haul your ass down to the station and really question you."

The sun began to set, slowly dipping over the horizon, dropping ever so slowly below the endless stretch of blue ocean. As it dropped, its color turned more orange than yellow. It seemed to sparkle. The air got cooler, people began to pack their things and prepare for that long journey home.

"Okay. I was there, that night but I didn't kill anybody if that's what you're thinking."

"Go on. I'm fascinated."

"I had a little unfinished business."

"Unfinished business. With Father Tim?"

"Father Tim?"

"Yeah. Father Tim. The guy, I mean, the priest that came to your apartment."

"Fuck no. My unfinished business was with the older guy. The pastor. I know the old guy hears confessions on Saturday night so I figured I'd drop in on him."

"Don't tell me. You were going to confess your sins. Reading porn magazines and watching porn movies and getting drunk and running down joggers. You were going to confess all that and return to the priesthood."

"Shit no. I had other business the that olf guy but I also was just going to tell him to keep that other priest out of my life. I waited a while until the church was empty and I opened his little curtain there."

"That's when you stabbed him, Father Tim. You were thinking it'd be the old priest and you see it's Father Tim, the priest you don't like, so you stabbed him."

"You have a vivid imagination, Roark. Now, can we go back to my apartment? I mean, can I go back to my apartment? I think I've said enough. Besides, you told me you were about to arrest my ex and all you needed was a little help from me."

"That's right, Jerry. I just wanted to clear the air and see if you were going to help me or not."

"That would really give me a hard-on, if I could help you do that."

"The knife, Jerry. She said you had a large knife, like one of those military things with a blade about this long," with his hands Roark showed a space of about six to eight inches, indicating the length of the blade.

"Jesus, Roark. Are you fucking kidding me? She said I had a knife like that? See. See what I mean. She's trying to pin this on me."

"The knife, Jerry. You had one or you didn't? Here's your chance. Maybe your last chance."

They walked in silence, now passing Santa Monica pier on their left. Roark waited patiently, didn't want to press the issue. He felt so close but he wanted it to come naturally out of Jerry's mouth.

"I haven't seen that knife in a long time. I have no idea where it went. And it pisses me off. My father gave it to me. So that's two things she stole from me, that statue and my goddamn knife."

"I can see you wanting the knife, Jablonski but why the statue. Thought you gave up religion."

"You're right, Roark. I don't give a shit about no statue. I just didn't want her to have it. But the knife, that's different."

Then Roark asked the key question, the one he'd been burning to ask, "Just for the record then. So, we know we're talking about the same knife. Describe it for me, Jerry. If you get it right, and you don't have it, that means she would have had it and that means she's the murderer."

Chapter Thirty-One

That made it clear. The knife. If Jablonski described it perfectly then the case is literally closed, thought Roark. Could this finally be the game-winning home run?

For obvious reasons the description of the knife had never been revealed to the public so now, if Jablonski describes it, Roark wins the game.

Just one problem. The knife Jablonski described didn't come close to matching that of the murder weapon. So, what conclusion should he draw from that, Roark asked himself.

If he was telling the truth then Jablonski, for the time being anyway, would be off the hook. If he was lying, he was lying for the obvious reason. Once again Roark was stymied and couldn't think of a way around it. Jablonski might be a horseshit guy but there's no crime in being a horseshit guy and Roark had to admit that he had absolutely no evidence to pin Jablonski.

There was just one loose thread. What on earth did Jablonski mean when he said he had some unfinished business with the old priest? When asked, Jablonski refused to answer. Said it was too embarrassing and had nothing to do with the murder.

Roark made an appointment to see Father Gregory one more time. Hopefully, this would be the last. He had to clear up that little matter of unfinished business that Jablonski had mentioned. At first, Father Gregory dodged him but, eventually, found time to see Roark.

Roark entered Father Gregory's office to find him busy packing.

"Going somewhere, Father?"

"I'm being transferred, Detective. Seems they want some new blood around here. What can I do for you, today?"

"I'm sorry to see you go."

Father Gregory looked up, grunted ever so slightly, then continued with his packing - books, paraphernalia, personal and religious items.

"You had a question, Detective Roark?"

"I've been interrogating a person of interest. The ex-husband of our fair Miss Kitty Meadows."

"Yes. And what does that have to do with me?"

"He seems to know you."

Father Gregory laughed, "Know me? Is that one of your jokes, Inspector Roark?"

"I'd like a straight answer."

"I have, at various times, over five hundred people in this parish. Maybe more. Certainly, Inspector Roark, you don't expect me to remember each and every one of them."

"It's just a little more than a coincidence. Father Tim is murdered by someone. The only witness is a young woman named Kitty Meadows whose husband just happens to know you. I am an investigator, Father, and the first commandment is I don't like coincidences. Things just don't happen out of chance. They happen for a reason."

"Like I said, Inspector. I have a lot of people in this parish. They could all say they know me," The old priest stopped packing and thought for a moment. Then he nodded.

"What?" Roark asked seeing something in the old priest's face that told him something significant was about to be unveiled.

"There was a young man I seem to recall. He came to the rectory. He was very upset. I told him I'd talk to Father Tim and see that the problem was resolved."

"That was it? Can you describe him? Do you remember his name?"

"Inspector Roark, please. You're asking me to remember the name of somebody I talked to weeks ago. I hardly remember where I park my car these days let alone the name of somebody that long ago."

Chapter Thirty-Two

In a moment of total frustration and helplessness, Roark decided to talk to Marvin, the pompous ass of a criminal psychologist, one more time. His first visit had produced absolutely nothing in Roark's estimation and that made Roark think this guy was just a charlatan feeding off the ignorance of the police department. If so, he sure had them fooled, including the noble commissioner who recommended him.

"Doctor Schofield, I was hoping you could shed some light on my investigation," Roark asked as respectfully as he possibly could be about anything. "You see, it's been two months since the murder and I haven't solved it yet. In fact, I don't have much of anything tangible to go on."

"I see you've come alone, Inspector. What happened to your partner?"

"He's off on another assignment. Besides, he's an asshole."

Schofield frowned, "I'm not real fond of language like that, Inspector. I think it's offensive."

"Murder's offensive, Marvin," Roark retorted, calling him by his given name.

"Yes, it is. So how can I help?"

"First of all, I've ruled out suicide. The victim had a lethal wound on the left side of his throat and, being left-handed, he would have had it on the right side of his throat." Roark demonstrated how that would look.

"I'll hold that thought, Detective. So, where does that leave you?"

"I've got a woman who I suspect could be lying through her teeth and very well might have been terribly involved with the victim in a romantic way and, because things turned sour, may have killed him."

"And why do you think that?"

"Oh, no reason at all. He got her pregnant and when she pressed him to live up to his responsibility and marry her; she killed him when he refused."

"And you know that to be true?"

"Actually, no. I don't. It came to me in a dream."

"Inspector? Really? That's all you have. A woman of sin, in a dream?"

"There's her ex-husband. Problem is I can't tie him to the murder victim. I don't see a motive there. He had opportunity and the means but no motive. If he's not the perp then it has to be the woman. I'm almost sure of it."

"Hmmnnnnn..." Schofield breathed. "Have you asked God for help in this matter?"

"Huh? I didn't know God was into criminal investigation. I thought he was busy enough doing other things than to get involved in this," Roark said derisively masking it as best he could not to offend Schofield too much while he needed the man's help. There would be ample time afterward to offend him, thought Roark.

"God, is the ultimate criminal investigator, Detective. He's the judge of us all. Who better to assist you than the one who knows all things?"

"Well, the problem is this. He hasn't spoken to me, lately. Not in the last ten years anyway."

"That's probably because you don't pray, Inspector."

Roark was losing patience, but he tried not to show it. He had to bite his tongue from saying things he really wanted to say. This man could really rattle his cage.

"I remember," he said finally, in a calm voice. "When I was a kid, I'd go to the Coliseum and watch the Rams play and whenever they were losing, I'd sit in the stands and pray my guts out that God would make the Rams win the game. Making my way back home, after another Ram's defeat, I'd wonder about my prayers. Why they weren't answered? Somewhere along the way, after this happened several times, it occurred to me why God hadn't answered my prayers."

"And what conclusion did you come to, Inspector?" Schofield asked in earnest, suddenly coming forward, resting his arms on his desk.

"I figured out there might just be some other stupid teenager on the other side of the stadium praying just as hard as I was for the other team to win. Even God can't make both teams win. So, He had to answer one prayer and deny the other."

"I don't think it's that simple, Inspector."

"I do. I think after years of thinking about this whole thing that God doesn't really answer prayers. I think it's nothing more than wishful thinking. If he did answer prayers, babies with cancer wouldn't die, people would all get the jobs they wanted, and every girl would be crowned Miss America."

"You ridicule and deny something that's very real, Inspector, the very thing that you don't believe in. God answers prayers. That much we know for sure. He doesn't always answer the prayer in the manner in which we want it to be answered but he does answer the prayer in one way or another."

"And you know this how?"

"Because, Inspector, I'm a man of faith and I read and study the Bible. It's all there. You just have to read it. I suspect you've never read it."

"Marvin, I appreciate the church lesson. I really do. But right now, I'd like to get to more concrete stuff involving my murder."

"If I may, Inspector. Let me repeat what I said before. I suspect the murder you are trying to solve has something to do with pedophiles. I have it on good authority that it's considerably more rampant than the Catholic Church or the news media let on. If you go back and take a look at the priest's history, I wouldn't be surprised at all if he had..."

"I think he was too much into women, Marvin, than to mess around with boys. Just my opinion."

Schofield smiled. "You don't believe in the Bible and prayer and you don't believe that I know a little more about the criminal mind than you do, Inspector. There's nothing terribly inconsistent with a man wanting sex from a woman or from a young boy, whatever at the moment, happens to be available. The key here is the need for gratification. The need to enjoy physicality. Let me pin it down for you, Inspector. Priests spend a lot of time in the church with young boys, young gullible, unsuspecting boys who firmly trust the priest, more so maybe than their own parents. He can do no wrong in their misguided minds. So, they concede. They do the awful thing that he urges them to do. Somehow, in their vulnerable state of mind they are able to rationalize that it's okay."

"You're forgetting one thing, Marvin. I was an altar boy once, before I grew out of it."

"And?"

"Not once did any of a dozen priests ever come close to getting personal with me."

Schofield then put his hands together, intertwining his fingers, deep in thought. "You may very well have been one of the lucky ones, Inspector. I suspect a lot of men, if asked to summon the courage to tell the truth, would have a different story."

"Well, Marvin. Thanks for lecture. I was hoping you'd have something more concrete than that. Pedophiles and prayer. I'll give that some thought. But, whatever." Roark paused. "Okay, here's a question of a different sort. Maybe we can keep the Bible out of it. The woman, the one I told you about before, she seems, on the one hand, guilty as hell. Just my sense of things. But, on the other hand, I can't imagine it being possible. She'd have to be lying about every blessed thing she's told me so far. Is that possible? Can she..."

Marvin folded his hands together intertwining the fingers so they pointed to the sky. He was beaming, like Roark had given him the perfect question. "She might very well, Inspector, be one of those people who, for whatever reason, have some difficulty telling the truth about anything. It's, for lack of a technical term I don't need to go into, a bit of a twisted mentality that fires the imagination. The person's imagination, in this instance, has a fascination with seeing the world differently than anyone else sees it. It's rare, but not that rare. You may have just found such a person. You're saying she lies about everything?”

“I think so.” Roark paused to reflect.

“The way you hesitate, I suspect, Inspector, you're either grasping at straws or, for some reason, you want to protect this woman. Would I be correct in thinking there might be some romantic interest on your part?”

Roark looked annoyed. “Absolutely not. This isn't about me, Marvin.”

Roark knew when to put an end to things. “Thanks for the visit and the information.” As he rose to leave, he added a question. “By the way, what happened to the picture of you and your family?”

Schofield turned around, annoyed. “We're in the process of getting a divorce. I put the picture away.”

“Maybe that's the real reason they were all smiling in the picture.”

Schofield looked up, halfway between anger and stupidity, not entirely sure of Roark's message. “Huh?”

As Roark was walking out of the office, Marvin gathered himself for one more comment.

“You were lucky, Roark. Maybe nothing happened to you in the church. But there are other places a lot more fertile for that kind of perverted activity.”

“Yeah? Where, Doc? Medical school?”

Schofield gave Roark a stern and parting look. "There's no better place than at the seminary where they all go to become priests. Think about it, Roark, what better place for that to happen than a private school tucked away, far from civilization, with just a handful of priests teaching hundreds of young gullible men, all in tight quarters, in a school I might add, where they eat, sleep, recreate, and maybe shower together."

"And you know this how?" Roark asked as sarcastically as he knew how.

"Like you, I nspector," he said with a mean look on his face, "I have my sources."

CHAPTER THIRTY-THREE

That just might be the missing motive. Maybe. It was a long shot, to be sure. Damn that Bible quoting asshole psychiatrist, he might be right. Right now, it was the only thing he had to go on. Either that or go back to casting Kitty Meadows as a wicked, conniving woman, worse than Delilah in the Bible, a woman capable of murder.

It had legs. Jablonski had said he studied to be a priest for a short time. It shouldn't be that hard to connect the dots between him and Father Tim. Maybe they were there at the same time. If so, that would tie them together for sure.

The lady ushered Roark into an office where he was greeted, much to his surprise, by a black priest. It wasn't just his race but something else Roark had not seen before.

"You're surprised, Inspector," the priest asked, seeing the look on Roark's face.

"I've never seen a black priest before, Father. Sorry."

"It's perfectly all right. I understand. Yes, in this part of the world we are a minority but, in other parts of the world, a white priest is in the minority."

"I'll have to take your word for that, Father. But there was something else that caught my eye."

"Yes?" The black priest asked.

"The red sash. Mighty fancy."

"You're very observant, Inspector, but it's not a fashion statement. It merely means I'm a monsignor which is just a little bit above being a regular priest. Kind of showy I'll admit. But it goes with the territory. Oh, and by the way, the answer is no, I did not play basketball in high school."

"You read my mind. By the way, I feel really stupid calling you Father or Monsignor when you're younger than I am. Believe me, I have all the respect in the world for the priesthood. I was once a Catholic so I respect that. It's just that..."

"What drove you away, Inspector, if I may ask?"

"It's a long story."

"I have time. Call me Dominic. I'd love to hear what happened."

"Sorry, Dominic. With all due respect, I'd like to get to the business I came here for."

"And what business would that be, Inspector?"

"The seminary. Where all you guys go to become priests. Where is this and how would I find out some things?"

"It's presently in Camarillo, Inspector. Why on earth would you want to know about that?"

"I have my reasons. Okay. I'm working on a murder. A priest got murdered a couple of months ago."

"Oh, yes. I sort of remember reading about it in the paper. I think they mentioned it on TV, too. Not that I watch TV very much but I was curious what happened. That was, what? A couple of months ago?"

"Something like that."

"Sad, very sad. But what does this have to with the seminary in Camarillo?"

"We think... I think ... the victim and one of my primary suspects may have been at this seminary at the same time."

"And, years later, one of them decided to kill the other? I don't get the connection, Inspector."

"I think it may be a case where one of them, you know, seduced the other. Or something like that."

The black priest sat down behind his desk, beckoning Roark to do the same in a chair on the opposite side of the desk. He looked sad.

"This is something that has hurt the Church very deeply. No question about it. Men and boys, in proximity of each other, too long, too often. Temptation overcomes will power. All these years, all these centuries, actually, priests have been looked up to as a guiding light, a father figure, if you will. Someone who could be trusted to help you and listen to your deep, dark secrets. In the confessional. Give out God's mercy and forgiveness. And now, something like this happens. It's awful. But, Inspector, let me assure you I don't believe it's as widespread as you might think, or the media might like you to believe. Sure, almost every month there's some news item about some priest in a parish where he gave in to temptation and now the parish is paying a sum of money damages to the victim. What you don't see is a news item that could and should be going out every day about the priests who honor their vow of chastity and do nothing wrong other than minister to their flock."

"Sounds like your background is in public relations, Dominic."

The priest laughed, a hearty, natural laugh. "Actually no, Inspector. I came from a poor family in the ghetto and...well, suffice it to say, I have no background in public relations but I understand why you were thinking that." He paused to reflect. "I think what you need to do, Inspector, is go to our seminary in Camarillo and see for yourself what goes on there. Talk to the instructors and staff. Some of them have been there for years and they may be able to help you. I wish I could help you but I can't. I have no knowledge of things of this nature. In Camarillo, they have everything there."

"Would they have pictures? And names?"

The black priest grinned. "Of course. The seminary is a licensed institution of higher learning, licensed by the state. By law, it must keep records and, along with that, it has yearbooks. I suspect you'll find everything in order."

Chapter Thirty-Four

Roark pondered driving to Camarillo. It was easily a good two hours drive, maybe more. Way out to the far reaches of the San Fernando Valley. And that's just driving time to get near the place. The way the black monsignor described it, finding it might be a little difficult too. He'd already gone to San Diego on a wild good chase and didn't relish the idea of repeating that mistake. But, what else could he do? Why not just call somebody out there? Roark dismissed the idea. It would pay to see the place.

Most of the time, when solving a crime, the answer has been the most simple, straight-forward answer. Complications and surprises only happen in the movies and on TV shows, Roark assured himself. Here he had, almost in his clutches, a really bad guy in Jablonski. He just needed some proof, some kind of tangible evidence tying him to Father Tim. A two hour drive out to the far reaches of the San Fernando Valley would be a small price to pay.

Most of the city of Los Angeles and surrounding suburbs is engulfed in a half Ushaped basin. On the west and south side, there's the ocean. On the north and east side there are mountains. When the industrial toxins get into the air and the ocean breezes blow inward, they push this toxic air east and trap it up against the mountains and the entrapment is what causes the smog. That and a gazillion cars driving up and down freeways all hours of the day and night.

To get to the San Fernando Valley from Los Angeles he had to drive over the pass to get from one basin to the other. It took him out of Los Angeles and dumped him into San Fernando Valley which, unlike much of the Los Angeles area, is nothing more than a desert. True, it no longer looked like a desert with all the housing tracts and green lawns and huge shopping centers but, nevertheless, it was a desert. If warm winds blow in the Los Angeles basin, they blow even warmer in the valley.

He drove up the tree lined road that led to the seminary. Monsignor Dominic's directions were excellent. Parking his car, he looked around but saw no one. It looked, for all he could see, like the place might be deserted. That only increased his belief that maybe the reason the seminary was this far away from heavily crowded Los Angeles and its immediate suburbs was so whatever was going on out here would stay out here.

He found an entrance to a building that looked like it might be an office. A priest was there, waiting to receive him. They shook hands and sat on facing leather chairs.

"I'm Father Metzger. I'm the one you spoke to on the phone. You said, Inspector, that you wanted to look at some old records? Might I ask, what it is you're trying to find? A murder investigation you said? I fail to see the connection. We've had no murders here."

When Roark made the appointment, he told the priest as little as he could get away with, leaving the priest totally in the dark. Now it was time to come clean. He said, "I think the man who killed a priest might have a connection to the priest, something that I think may have started here."

"And that connection would be?"

"He studied to be a priest, so he said anyway. I need to check that out and see if maybe the two of them were in the same group or the same class. Maybe some connection. That's where I was hoping you could fill in the blanks, Father."

"Oh dear, he studied for the priesthood? And you think he murdered a priest? That's an extremely sad state of affairs, Inspector."

"Murder usually is."

The priest smiled, "I understand that part of it but I just have some serious doubts."

"Fair enough, Father but could we start looking at some records?"

"The names of these two?"

"The victim was a priest by the name of Timothy Hanrahan. At least that's what the pastor told me."

"And the other man?"

"Jerry Jablonski. Again, I have no assurance that's his real name. All I have to go on is what he told me."

"What year would these two men have been here?"

"That's the part I don't know."

"Inspector, at any given time, we might have as many as three to four hundred or more students here. It would help if you had an idea."

"You don't keep an alphabetical listing of the students?"

"Yes, we do, but it's by year. It's not one great big list."

"Father Tim was around thirty-five or so. Jerry Jablonski would be about the same age. Does that help?"

"When a priest graduates and becomes ordained he is generally around twenty-five or twenty-six years old, some younger, some older. Assuming he was the normal age, that would mean he graduated anywhere over ten years ago. Perhaps we should start there, the late sixties and early seventies."

The priest led Roark to another office which contained old filing cabinets and in-

side were files and files, most needing dust-
ing. He opened one drawer, then another,
shutting each one in turn as he decided
that was not the right drawer. "I'm afraid we
need to go to our storeroom, Inspector."

"Lead the way, Father. By the way, where
is everybody? It's like a morgue around here
or is everybody on vacation?"

"Presently, they are at prayer, Inspector.
Soon they're scheduled to have lunch. I
made our appointment during this time so
we wouldn't be disturbed."

Roark nodded his understanding.

Inside the storeroom were boxes, the kind
people usually use when they're moving,
lock, stock, and barrel. They were all labeled with some kind of short description.
"You'll have to forgive me, Inspector. I've only been here five years and so I don't quite
know where everything is."

Unwrapping boxes that were wrapped
with cords was a task and it seemed like it
took forever. Finally, the priest found records that he thought would be helpful.
"Aha, I think this might help," he said.
"They are the lists of the entire student
body for those years, each in its own leather
pouch, year by year, it would appear. I'm
sorry, I don't think there's any better information. We'll just have to go through each
pouch and see what we can see. And, look
here, inspector. See these?" he said, pulling
out what looked like a picture album. "The-

se would be the photos of the entire student body and all the priests on staff. All you have to do is go through them."

Roark demurred, "I think I'd rather take these back with me and have some people help me go through them."

"I hate to give them up, Inspector. Any chance you could..."

"Father, I can assure you. They will be safe and will be returned intact, just the way you have them now. I can get a warrant, if necessary."

"Inspector, please. That won't be necessary. You may take whatever you wish, I just wanted to be sure, well, you know."

"Okay. So, you said you've only been here five years. Anybody here that might have been here ten to fifteen years ago?"

"Let me think. Yes. Father Flannigan has been here, I think, since the place opened."

"Is he here?"

"He would be at prayer or lunch."

"Anybody else? I think I'd like to talk to him or anybody else that might have been here. I drove a long way so I'd like to talk to whoever it might be."

"Well, let's see. Father O'Brien has been here a long time. Oh, and Father Sheridan. And I believe Father O'Reilly has been here that long."

"Sounds like the Irish Mafia, if you ask me," Roark said in a joking manner.

Father Metzger laughed. "You know, Inspector, sometimes I'm inclined to think you might be right. These Irish priests are sometimes a strange, stubborn lot. I'll ask each of them to come to the office. Do you want them one by one or all together?"

Roark was tired. Tired of talking to people and getting nowhere. Tired of driving to Camarillo and the thought of driving back made him even more tired than normal. And now he had ten boxes of files to go through when he got home.

As a group they had been quite pleasant and cooperative, almost delighted to talk about the history of the seminary and their part in it. But they also seemed to be quite naive and unusually innocent of the ways of the world; his world anyway. When Roark suggested there might have been a physical connection between fellow students Timothy Hanrahan and Jerry Jablonski one of them actually asked what sort of physical connection did he have in mind. The other three just seemed to go into disbelieving shock mode, looking at each other wondering what anybody knew. They then, in turn, vowed they were not aware of anything of the sort. The worst part was none of the four remembered either Timothy Hanrahan or Jerry Jablonski. Roark sighed.

The ten boxes just barely fit in the back seat and trunk of his car. Another wasted trip, he thought to himself. No doubt he'd need help looking through the boxes but taking them to the office would be a pain. He'd look like a fool. That meant taking them to his apartment. Still, some help would be needed. Culpepper?. "Christ," he ground his teeth. "In my apartment?" he said out loud. "No way, Jose. So now what?"

Then it occurred to him. There was such a person who could help him. What better person could there be to identify Hanrahan and Jablonski? What other person was there on earth that knew them more intimately?

CHAPTER THIRTY-FIVE

"I thought you didn't believe me, Inspector Roark." Kitty said to Roark when he called her.

"Let's say I've had a change of heart. So how about it? You up for helping me? And what's with the Inspector Roark? I thought we were on a first name basis."

"It seems a bit unfair. You not trusting me yet you want my help."

"I think I'd trust you a lot better if you helped me. I'll supply the wine."

"Okay. I'll be there tomorrow night after work."

"Why don't I pick you up?"

"I think, Sebastian, at this point I'd prefer to have my own transportation rather than being totally dependent upon you to get me home safely."

Like two teenagers they sat on the floor of his apartment, cross-legged, each one working on a box and sipping wine "That's a big bottle of wine," she said when he showed it to her.

"We got a lot of work to do."

"These are the only wine glasses you have?" She teased him when she saw he brought out two glasses that resembled what a child would use to drink milk out of.

"Sorry. I ran out of paper cups."

Laboriously, they went through the box with the oldest records then worked forward towards later years.

Halfway through, she said. "I'm hungry."

"I'll order pizza," Roark snorted.

"Nonsense. I'll cook something."

"I didn't bring you over here to cook."

"You didn't bring me over here at all. I drove myself, remember?"

"Yeah, you drove. I'll order pizza."

She was already out of the sitting position and leaping into the kitchen before he could stop her. Opening the refrigerator door, she growled. "There's nothing in here but beer and milk." Then opening and slamming shut kitchen cabinets, she shrieked. "You have absolutely nothing in this kitchen."

"There's frozen food things in the freezer."

"Yuk. I don't eat frozen food. You know what junk they put in those? You'd be better off eating the cardboard carton they come in."

Roark grunted. "I'll order a pizza."

They drank more wine and ate the pizza. They started to get silly and there remained, roughly, two more years of boxes.

Roark asked Kitty. "You haven't seen any trace of the name Jablonski?"

"Nope," she said starting to sound inebriated.

"How about the pictures? No sign of him or Father Tim?"

"Right now, they're all are starting to...to look alike. Faces and more faces."

Up until this point, the search for two names and two pictures was going nowhere. Then she asked him, "Is this what you're looking for?"

Roark squinted into an album she was holding. To do that, he had to get close, real close. Her perfume filled his nostrils. He paused, longer than was necessary, to look at the name she had found.

"No. That's Hannity. Not Hanrahan."

"Oh," she said, putting her hand up in front of her face, followed by a girlish giggle, nurtured by too much wine. "Is this what people mean when they say they're looking for a needle in a haystack?"

Roark decided. "Okay, I think we need to stop. We'll finish tomorrow or the next day or whatever."

"You're going to drag me over here again, Sebastian? If I didn't know any better, I'd think you're trying to get me drunk and then have your way with me."

"Kitty. Please. Enough. Okay? You might think this is fun and games but this is work for me, serious work."

"You always work in your apartment with a giant bottle of wine?"

"I thought maybe..."

"What?"

"I thought maybe...; I don't know what I was thinking," Roark said...

"You still don't trust me."

Roark knew he, too, was beginning to lose it. The bottle of wine was almost gone. A three to four-hour round trip to Camarillo, lugging boxes of records in his car, and way too much wine. A beautiful woman in his apartment.

She might be his Delilah, like in the movie, considerably cleverer than she pretended to be. He'd gone to the bathroom once to urinate. Maybe while he was gone, she could have slipped something into his drink? Just like Delilah did with poor, unsuspecting Sampson?

Oh God, he thought. How did I let this happen?

She was the first to get up, preparing to leave but she wobbled with her first step, almost falling over the coffee table. "Whoa," she said. "That's not good."

He noticed her condition. "I don't think you're going anywhere."

"I have to." She braced herself against the door that would have let her out of the apartment. She paused. "But then again, I think maybe I'd better not. No way am I driving. No way am I going anywhere."

Chapter Thirty-Six

He awoke with a ray of the morning sun shining in his eyes. Usually, last thing at night, he'd shut the curtains but he hadn't done so last night. He lay there, blinking his eyes, trying to get them to focus. He had the sudden realization he was naked. He glanced over to his left. She was there, facing in the opposite direction, her bare shoulders and upper back visible above the covers.

Oh my god, thought Roark. What have I done? Suddenly, all the various possibilities attacked his brain like creatures from outer space. He'd had sex with a person of interest in a murder case. Hopefully, he thought, someone that he was no longer investigating if it was ever found out by his superiors. Like millions of other men, he had succumbed to temptation. A beautiful woman and too much alcohol. He felt foolish and stupid. Then his thoughts turned to how to cover this up and put it behind him. All this time, he thought he was too smart to fall into a trap like this. Sampson and Delilah? All over again.

He felt on top of his head to see if he still had his hair, remembering that poor Sampson lost his. Ah, fortunately, it was all there. Now, how was he going to get her dressed and out of his apartment?

For some strange, totally illogical reason, he felt embarrassed, embarrassed at his own nakedness and being in a room with a naked lady. Quickly, before she awoke, he slipped out of bed and got dressed in some pants and a shirt, flattened down his hair with water in the bathroom and slipped out of the room.

Within minutes, herself fully dressed, she followed him into the living room. They looked at each other sheepishly and then they both glanced around the room. It was a bit of a mess, a very large and now empty wine bottle, two drinking glasses and a pizza carton left wide open. Two pieces of cold pizza remained and they stunk up the room.

"You left in a hurry," she said.

"I thought you might like some privacy to get dressed."

She smiled, turning a little red. She checked all her buttons and bows to see that she was fully dressed. "I guess I better go."

"You want coffee."

"No, I think I better go."

He detected her dissatisfaction with something, more than likely with what had happened the night before. He was strongly motivated to break into a full explanation of sorts but couldn't think of anything to say other than something trite.

"I'm sorry about last night. It shouldn't have happened."

She moved toward the door to make her exit and they exchanged meaningful glances.

"Don't be. It wasn't any more your fault than it was mine."

"But I..." Then she shushed him up, putting her finger to his lips.

"It's all right. Let's just forget it ever happened."

"It wasn't supposed to," he agreed.

She was at the door and turned to give him one last look. "At least you tried. That's all a girl can ask for."

Chapter Thirty-Seven

Two boxes of records remained. He could handle that all by himself. No reason to get her involved any more. He wasn't really too sure now that he had time to think about whether or not she really had her heart in it. How did he know, for example, whether she saw a face or a name that was familiar and just deliberately passed over it? For him, that meant he had a decision to make. Either go through the boxes she had looked in again, just to make sure, or assume, as hard as that might be at the moment, that she was doing her best.

It was as equally frustrating going through the last two boxes as it had been the previous night. Then it dawned on him that even if he found Father Tim and Jerry Jablonski on a list in the same group and an accompanying photo hugging each other in an embarrassing embrace, it wouldn't prove a thing. Maybe the whole exercise was tantamount to nothing. Maybe he was grasping at straws or worse yet, pissing into the wind. He set the boxes aside.

He went into the office. Hardly anyone was there on a Sunday. Maybe, he thought, it was time to give it up and leave it as an unsolved murder. Wouldn't be the first time that happened. In the chronicles of criminal prosecution there were many unsolved crimes and some of them became famous because of that very fact.

What was he doing in the office on a Sunday, he asked himself after wasting several minutes looking around his desk, checking his in-basket and answering machine for messages? Nothing reached the level of importance he was hoping for. Why was he not at home, in his apartment, sitting at his card table, rearranging his notes?

The answer came to Roark like a shock of stark reality. He felt uncomfortable in his own apartment. On the one side it was awfully lonely with nothing there but a card table with notes and ten boxes of files. He hardly ever watched TV unless he expected local news coverage regarding a crime that had recently been committed. It was always interesting to him how the media seemed to totally confuse the real issues. Needless to say, they could only go by what information they were given by law enforcement and, to be sure, that was about as reliable and revealing as a fortune teller predicting the end of one's love life. Still, you'd think they'd just report what they knew, not what they suspected might be true. That's why his classic answer to any news media person was to indicate it's an investigation that's still underway and he's not at liberty to reveal any further information. That pat answer circulated around the local news media leaving him a very poor target for questioning and, to be sure, that's exactly how he liked it. He wasn't bucking to make police commissioner much less, running for public office, so there was no need to see his face on TV or his name in the newspaper.

On the other hand, the apartment was no longer a sacred place to hide...no longer his cave, or safety zone. She had been there, not for just a quick visit but to purposefully invade his space. She had opened his refrigerator, criticized his inventory of food, made fun of his poor collection of proper wine glasses and worst of all, had slept in his bed. Roark wondered what it would be like, night after night, sleeping in that bed without her. How many times would he think about that, trying in vain to go to sleep? Damn women; they get in your head. They screw up a man's life. The only solution was to move. That apartment would never be the same. Whenever he'd use it as his man-cave or safety blanket he'd remember her being there.

Before going home, he paid one more visit to Jablonski. Hopefully it'd be a worthwhile little visit.

"Working on Sunday, Roark? How noble. I'm impressed. I suppose you want to come in."

"I'm surprised you're still here, Jablonski. I sort of figured you'd be fleeing out of the state by now."

"Fleeing? And why would I do that?"

"Oh, I don't know. Maybe being the prime suspect in a murder investigation might cause you to want to get out of town."

"I didn't know I was your prime suspect."

"You're right up there at the top of the list, buddy boy."

"How many other people are on this list of yours."

"Right now, just one. That's you."

"You said she was at the top of your list and all you needed to nail her was my help. Anyway, where the fuck would I go? No money; no job. At least this apartment is paid for till the end of the month. I suppose I could become one of them homeless people in San Francisco and sleep in the park with all the weirdoes and gays. Besides, I know you'd track me down."

Roark said nothing, instead, he studied Jablonski intently, listening carefully to every word. Looking and hoping for him to screw up and say something self-incriminating. Criminals do that, Roark re-assured himself. They do it for a number of reasons. First of all, criminals are generally not the brightest people on the planet and they sometimes say dumb things. The other reason is they often want, desperately, to confess. The crime wears heavily on their minds. It often keeps them awake at night, tormenting them. So, they want to get caught. After all, it's their moment in the spotlight. They'll be on the nightly news, maybe get their picture in the paper. In Jablonski's case, thought Roark, he might even see it as a better way of life. A life in prison with no worries about finding a job, three square meals a day, and a permanent roof over his head. No problems with women, replaced by daily card games, TV, maybe even a few porn magazines.

"I got one question for you, Jablonski. What year were you studying to be a priest?"

Jablonski smiled. It was an evil smile in Roark's estimation.

"You looking for me to give you some rope to hang me with?"

"It's a simple question, Jablonski. I can easily get the answer by calling the right people but I just thought maybe, since you've got nothing to hide, that you'd save me some time."

"1970."

Roark's mind rotated like a Vegas slot machine. 1970...that was the earliest year Father Metzger had given him for the range in which they might find Jablonski's name and photo. But they'd already looked at that first year. He and Kitty Meadows. Damn her. That was her year. She's the one who looked through that box. He had elected to take 1971. No reason. He just picked it.

"You sure about that, Jablonski? Remember, I'll find out if you're lying."

With renewed energy and resolve he headed back to his apartment forgetting for the moment that he'd find a skeleton of recent bad memories there. And Kitty Meadows? She was going to catch hell from him. Beautiful or not beautiful, she was going to pay for messing around with him, and playing him for a fool.

Chapter Thirty-Eight

Bounding up the steps to get to his second-floor apartment, he couldn't wait to bust open the box for 1970. Then, he'd confront Kitty Meadows. He'd get to the bottom of this crime if it's the last thing he ever did. The figure he saw sitting in front of his apartment was the last figure he expected to see.

"What the hell are you doing here?" He asked Kitty.

Startled, she jumped up to face him. "I knew you had to come home sooner or later."

"You could have called. I would have saved you a trip."

"You never gave me your number."

"Never thought I needed to. What's in the bag?" He asked, noticing for the first time she had what looked like a grocery bag, large enough to include a change of clothes.

"I brought us some dinner. I cooked it myself. All we need do is heat it up. You have a microwave, don't you?"

"You said 'us'. You were planning for us to dine together?"

She looked surprised. "You didn't expect me to eat pizza two times in a row, did you?"

Roark eyed the bag suspiciously. Then he eyed her suspiciously. What the hell was she doing here? "Dinner. Okay. But nothing else."

She smiled then appeared hurt. "I thought we'd finish those two boxes."

"I don't need your help. I can finish them myself."

She pouted with her lower lip curling up over her upper lip. To Roark, she genuinely looked disappointed and hurt. When women did that sort of thing, he was a sucker for it.

"Well, if that's the way you want it. Then let's eat."

With all the precision of a master chef she had the bag she brought emptied and the inner contents poured onto a cooking dish. She next turned to the oven with Roark standing there. "Can you set it for 350?" She asked.

He looked, dumbfounded. "Set the oven? Why? The microwave's right there."

"I prefer the oven, if you don't mind." She insisted.

"Can't do that," he reiterated.

"Is it broken?"

"I don't know. I've never used it."

She brushed him aside, in a playful manner, her breasts grazing against his upper arm as she went by. She lit the oven and

Roark threw his hands up in mock surrender.

"Okay. Have it your way. While we wait, do me one favor, will you? Look at the box for 1970 again. See if you see your ex-husband in the picture with his name on the list."

"Why 1970? I did that last night."

"Do it again."

"What's the magic word?"

He shook his head in total frustration. "Please?"

She went immediately to the box and opened its contents. Going to the list she went through each grade and then looked at each picture. After what seemed like a long time she looked up, looking totally helpless and frustrated. "I don't see him. Did you think he was there, in 1970?"

"Are you sure?"

"Yes. Look again. You may have missed his name or his picture. He might not have been in the picture. He may have changed between the time the picture was taken and you knew him"

"Could we eat dinner first? I'm hungry."

Out of the oven came the baking dish out of which she scooped two servings of a casserole dish into bowls she found in the cabinet, giving him the lion's portion.

Roark looked at it. "What is this?"

"A nice casserole. And it's very healthy. I made it special, for you."

He stirred around in the bowl with a fork. Where's the meat?"

"There is no meat. It's meatless."

"Meatless?" He said unbelievingly. "Meatless?"

"It's loaded with veggies that have lots of vitamins."

Roark was sunk. No alternative. Begrudgingly, he ate the stew, in silence. She did likewise.

"Okay, he said. "Look again at 1970."

She looked at the first list, then another. She looked at the class picture of one of the grades, then another. The third picture she looked at, she moaned.

"What?" Roark asked impatiently.

"It's him." And she went silent.

"Father Tim?" Roark asked with renewed enthusiasm.

"No." My ex-husband. Jerry."

"Why didn't you catch that when you looked last night? It was the first box you opened."

"I don't know. You've seen him, right? Now he has long hair. I wasn't expecting to see him with short hair all nice and neat."

"Okay, I get that. Now. How about looking again and see if you see Father Tim."

She shook her head and folded her arms.

"What?" He asked.

"I don't want to do that. I can't," she said shaking her head again. "It's just too painful."

"Too painful? Really." Then he stopped, rubbing his chin, deep in thought. Was this the right time to ask, he wondered. What the hell.

"Too painful because you and he had sexual relations?"

She looked away and he could tell she was in great pain. This told him everything he thought he wanted to know.

She blurted. "Yes. You had to ask. You couldn't just leave it alone. You had to ask. So now I've told you. What of it? I don't suppose you'd understand but it was beautiful. It was special."

"What?" Roark slapped himself up side head. "You're telling me this now, after all this time? Why didn't you tell me before?"

"I couldn't," she pleaded.

"You couldn't and why the hell not? It's a simple question. Did you have sexual relations with Father Tim. You're fucking answer would have been 'yes'. One simple word. That's all it would've taken."

She began to moan, in a silent cry of agony. He patted her shoulder as if to tell her it was all right. "Tell me everything. Everything, and I mean it or it's going to be a long night.

Chapter Thirty-Nine

After she left his apartment he was left with the boxes. No Father Tim in the picture; just Jablonski. That was some measure of progress and, oh yes, her admission that they had been lovers. Jealousy? Screw it, he thought.

He stared at the boxes, incapable of moving. He had to admit he was nowhere on the case, absolutely nowhere. After four months he was absolutely nowhere.

Jablonski was in the seminary, just like he said. Father Tim and Kitty were lovers. What on God's green earth did any of this prove?

The thing that really bothered him was the fact she had lied to him. Goddamn women, he thought. They lie. Was she like one of those people that Schofield had described? Pathological liars? It comes so easy to them, Schofield had said. They become enchantingly good at it and it becomes a way of life.

But then, everybody lies. Maybe, he thought, he should get into another profession where people tell the truth. At the moment, however, he couldn't think of what profession that might be. Maybe he had heard so many lies over the years he could no longer recognize the truth if it slapped him upside the head. He had such a full litany of lies; he had them all memorized. He laughed out loud. "Maybe I should go into politics."

Before she left, after wiping away tears, and listening to his threats, she let it all go. It was like a waterfall of truth gushing over a cliff.

In the end, what did it matter? Two people, for a moment in time, doing something the man later regretted; something the woman cherished, perhaps for the rest of her life. What did it matter? He shrugged his shoulders. It probably had nothing to do with the murder so why dwell on it anymore?

Wistfully, he picked up the 1970 album and looked at the picture, one more time, staring at the man she picked out as Jablonski. Sure enough, other than the hair, he hadn't changed all that much in ten years.

Then he looked at the priests who were also in the picture, hoping, for no reason at all, to see one or more of them that he'd talked to when he went to Camarillo. That wasn't so easy. Ten years hadn't been so kind to these men or they just weren't there, in that picture.

Then he saw it.

He scrambled to his notes on the card table. What did Jablonski say? Unfinished business with the old priest?

CHAPTER FORTY

Time to talk to Father Gregory once again. He had something new to tell him and that thought delighted him. How could the pastor not know that Father Tim was having an affair? Christ, they lived together. Don't priests ever talk to each other? Confession. Yes. Besides, the picture in the book, in 1970. It was hard to tell because it was an old picture and people's faces do change over the course of ten years or so but it sure looked every bit like Father Gregory, in the same picture as Jablonski. That didn't prove a thing but it sure made him curious. Coincidence or was there something there that needed looking into?

"Thank you for seeing me, Father."

"It's been awhile, Inspector. I assume you're here because you have some new information on the case or am I correct in thinking the case has been solved? Please don't tell me our dear Father Tim's murder will go unsolved. That, Inspector, would be most unsettling. It could very well mean that we're all at risk. Do you know what I mean?"

"I do," said Roark, sitting quietly, perfectly willing to let Father Gregory vent and perhaps reveal something.

"These pedophile cases. They've got us all spooked. Think about it, Inspector. Some guy who's now about thirty years old, he reads in the paper that the Catholic Church has paid X amount of dollars in satisfaction of alleged acts of pedophilia. He decides he wants some of that money. The Church doesn't need the bad press or the aggravation. They concede and give the guy a tidy sum even though his claim may be entirely false. Or, worse yet. take the case of a guy thirty or so who really was abused as an altar boy when he was, say, twelve years old. He's lived with it all his life, not telling anybody. He's tormented by it, night and day. He's afraid to come forward and accuse the priest because he doesn't want the notoriety. He doesn't want it to come out that he was a victim. His family and friends, they might think he's lying or, if not, that he's awfully stupid for having let himself be abused. What kind of a person lets himself be abused? So, he lives with it, hoping to forget, but it won't go away. He's afraid to file a claim but wants the torment to end. He goes off the deep end and decides to kill himself or the priest who abused him. Or, worse yet, he decides to kill any priest, like it doesn't matter to him who really did it,

it's a matter of revenge against the priesthood and the Church."

"You worried, Father Gregory?"

"Ah, Inspector. Your mind is always
churning, always looking for ways to spin
around anything I say."

"You brought it up."

"Yes, I did. So, tell me. Why the visit?"

"I believe you said you did you know Father Tim was having an affair?"

"Yes. Yes, I think I said that."

Funny, he didn't hesitate for a moment,
thought Roark. "And?"

"I told him to put an end to it or I'd have
to turn him in to the Archdiocese. He promised me he would."

"Seems to me a transgression like that
deserves to be reported and punished. I'm
surprised."

"Forgiveness is part of the Church's phi-
losophy, Inspector. That's what it's all
about. When Christ came down and, well,
you know all about that. Forgiveness. That's
what we do."

"But is it your job to make that decision?"

"What are you asking me?"

"I'm asking if you have the authority to
look the other way or is having an affair
something that needs to be reported?"

"I didn't want to ruin a man's life, Inspector."

"Or harm the Church's reputation."

"You can be very annoying, Inspector. The Church's reputation is, no question, very important but, it's not worth ruining a man's life."

"I get that. I really do," Roark answered. Then he pursed his lips, deep in thought.

"Something else on your mind, Inspector?"

"I was just thinking. What if, instead of having an affair, Father Tim had sexually abused one of the altar boys? Would your position be the same? Tell him to stop? Ask for forgiveness, then cover it up?"

If Father Gregory was offended, he hid it well, showing little or no expression, just a bit of concern, a thoughtful look on his face. "Trying to catch me in a dilemma, Inspector? Trust me, this is why I enjoy our little visits. As I said before, as a priest I spend most of my time talking to people about their problems and it's never very cerebral but, with you, Inspector, it's very cerebral. I can almost see the wheels of suspicion grinding in your head."

"Then answer the question."

"I would give you the same answer. Under the Church's law both acts are a sin against God. Both can be forgiven if the person truly repents. I know what you're going to say. Having an affair is a not a crime under civil law, whereas abusing an underage child is." He stopped to rearrange himself in his chair and, perhaps, steal some time for additional thoughts. "Like I said before, I wouldn't want to ruin a man's life over one transgression."

"So, you wouldn't report it to the civil authorities."

"I couldn't."

"Why not?"

"The seal of confession. You know that, Inspector."

"What if you discovered it outside of confession?"

"There's no question," Father Gregory said, putting his hands together under his chin, as if in prayer. "It's a horrible thing to do to a child. But, hurting the Church's reputation is a horrible thing too. Millions of people depend on the Church for solace, for comfort, for the very salvation of their immortal souls. Why ruin that for them because of an isolated act that has no bearing whatsoever on the Church's teaching or its validity or its mission?"

"At the price of a life of mental anguish that the victim must endure."

"The victim needs to move on. Needs to forgive and forget. The only reason they bring it up years later is to get money. How does that remove the mental anguish?"

"If nothing else it brings to light a sickness in the Church that it hides from the public. By making it public, maybe, just maybe you guys would keep your hands off innocent altar boys."

Very much now irritated, Father Gregory said, rather emphatically and conclusively, "Although I don't entirely agree with it, Inspector, I do respect your opinion. Now are we done?"

"Did Father Tim molest any young boys? Yes or no?"

"You know I can't answer that, Inspector. Well, let me just say this. Not to my knowledge."

"Did you ever abuse any young boys?"

"Okay, Inspector, that's enough. As I said, I enjoy our conversations but you've gone too far. Is there anything else?"

"I see you taught up in Camarillo."

"And your point is?"

"Around all those good-looking young men. That had to be tempting. Way up there, far away from the big city."

"I feel sorry for you, Inspector. I really do. You live in a dark world where, because of your profession, you see nothing but evil, the worst mankind has to offer and you suspect everyone. That's a lot of evil. Your whole life is surrounded by evil. I understand you must ask questions and you have your right to be suspicious but you have severely insulted me. I have never. Let me repeat that. I have never laid my hands in a sexual way upon anyone."

"Then explain to me, Father Gregory. And, remember, you're sworn to tell the truth by your ordination, right? In the presence of

God, you must tell the truth. Why did Father Tim need to be killed?"

"I honestly don't know, Inspector. I wish I did. I would tell you."

"Okay. Tell me this. When I was last talking to the ex-husband of Kitty Meadows, he told me he had some unfinished business with you and it was too embarrassing for him to talk about it to me. C'mon, Father, come clean. What was that all about? And please don't say you have no idea or you can't remember him."

Father Gregory looked very grave, like he'd been told he had a terminal illness. He started to reach for his cigarettes or maybe the wine bottle, then slammed the drawer shut.

"It's not something I'm very proud of, Inspector. In fact, it haunts me all the time. You bringing it up, really hurts. Yes, I was there in 1970 and, yes, I remember the fellow you are referring to."

He paused to think and took just enough time for Roark's mind to salivate. This is it, his mind told him. Gregory is about to confess.

"I couldn't help myself. It just happened and not proud of it. I just happened to be walking around the shower area and I saw him. He was doing something that he shouldn't be doing, something I'm afraid young men do all the time. I told him he should be ashamed of himself and I thought that would be the end of it. But it wasn't. He actually mouthed off to me. I think it was a simple matter of he was angry and he was embarrassed and he had no other recourse. So, he mouthed off to me, like no other seminarian ever had."

"And?"

"I did what I had been trained to do for years. I hit him. Open handed, mind you. I didn't knock him unconscious or anything like that. I just reacted. I guess I still had that good, quick right hand. Still, I've been sorry for it ever since that day."

"Thought you said, last time we talked, you never boxed again after that black kid beat the shit out of you."

"Ah, inspector. You don't miss a thing, do you? Anyway, that was what this fellow probably meant by his unfinished business."

"He wanted a rematch? Duke it out with you?"

"No. Not at all. He wanted money. Said he was going to report me to the Archdiocese. I told him to go right ahead and do that and I'd suffer the consequences, whatever they might be."

"Did you give him money?"

"That, Inspector, is my business. As you know, we priest don't have much money and..." Then he stopped talking like his voice box had run out of air.

"I'll take that as a yes."

CHAPTER FORTY-ONE

Culpepper was back at it again, up to his old tricks. "Hey, Sebastian, we got a real problem here."

"Yeah. What do you mean we have a problem?"

"That guy, Jerry, you asked me to keep an eye on. He spotted me last night. Actually walked over to me as I was getting off my bike and introduced himself."

"Remind me, Roy boy, to never send you out again on surveillance. You had the perfect disguise. A space cadet. So, what happened?"

"He asked me to come up to his apartment. He wanted to show me something."

"You're kidding?"

"No. Why would I kid about a thing like that?"

"Did you go up to his apartment?"

"Sure, why not? I figured it might lead to a clue who killed that priest."

"Don't tell me, Roy boy, he showed you a knife that matches the one that he used to kill the priest and he then confessed and put his hands behind his back and begged you to cuff him. Did you read him his Miranda rights?"

"Shit, Sebastian. You're putting me on. No, it wasn't like that at all."

"Well then? What the fuck did he show you?"

"His apartment. He showed me how nice and clean it was. He showed me he got rid of all the porn magazines."

"That's it?"

"He asked me to give you a message. He said he got a job and he's cleaned up his act. He said he knew you were having him watched because you suspected he might skip town and he said you can forget it. He ain't skipping town because he had nothing to do with the murder. Since he got a job and cleaned up he said for me to pass along to you the best news."

"The best news? And what, exactly, might that be?"

"He said he got a bunch of money from some guy who owed it to him. He said he knew you'd be pleased to hear that."

Culpepper seemed extremely pleased with himself having accomplished, in his mind anyway, a major break in the case. Through careful scrutiny and careful surveillance, he had been the one able to clear up one of the suspects. Now it was up to Roark to finish the job.

Roark was speechless. He couldn't think of an intelligent thing to say. Or, an unintelligent thing either. He muttered the first words that came out of his mouth. "Nice work, Roy. Really. Nice work. I knew I could count on you."

Roark then weighed his alternative courses of action. He could either hang Culpepper by his balls or give up his job as a detective and go back to work as a night watchman or something that was brainless and would allow him to sleep at night. At this precise moment, he admitted to himself, that he was tired of policing. It was a thankless task. He was tired of asking people questions, tired of chasing leads that reached a dead end more often than not. Pity that his last case would be one that he failed to solve.

So, what was the best thing to do? Walk into the Commissioner's office and quit on the spot? Or, should he, instead, maybe draft a memo and put in the interoffice mail routing system? He could move to another city, get away from the smog and heat of Los Angeles. Get away from traffic pile-ups and plastic people.

Then a brilliant thought entered his head. Maybe Kitty Meadows would go with him. He was convinced she had a thing for him. Why else would she have so readily gone to bed with him a few nights ago? She's a poor soul who needed a change of scenery just as much as he did.

He got up from his desk, ready to go home and give all this some additional thought, a lot of thought.

His phone rang. He was tempted to not answer it but curiosity got the best of him. "Roark," he replied in a gruff but professional voice.

"Are you the person who is investigating the murder of that priest?" The voice was faint, an old lady's voice.

"Who is this?"

"I just had to call and say something."

"Lady, that was close to four months ago. Why now, after all this time, are you asking me about the case?"

There was a prolonged silence on the phone. He could tell the other person was struggling with an answer to the question. She finally replied. "I didn't think it meant anything so I just didn't bother."

"What?"

"I saw who might have murdered Father Tim."

Chapter Forty-Two

Roark hung up the phone and his mind went into overdrive. What the hell should he make of this? Why now, after four months? Another wild goose-chase? No question, it was legendary how people come forward with some theory of a crime. Why do they do it? Sometimes they're just lonely and want to talk to somebody and what they have to say turns out to be nothing. Sometimes they have the best of motives but they misunderstand things or they get things just plain wrong. In most cases, it turns out that their story is useless.

But this might be different. This was not just an ordinary person who just happened to see the bulletin asking for help and sat on it for almost four months. This was a person who was right there, in the middle of things.

He felt really foolish after hanging up the phone. All those thoughts of retiring and taking Kitty Meadows to a new location were as far out of his mind now as a distant planet.

His immediate reaction was the normal one, the one that so easily came to his mind. Father Gregory was now back in play.

As was his custom and favorite routine, he suggested coming over immediately to her house and she was so appreciative of that she couldn't stop thanking him enough. "Thank you so much, Mr. Roark. You know I don't like going out much anymore. It's just too difficult for me. The doctors have told me I shouldn't drive and I'm..."

"It's okay. Stay right there. I'll be there in fifteen minutes."

Hers was an old tear down halfway to Santa Monica and a little south. Towards the airport. One of what seemed like millions of postwar houses built when the soldiers came home from World War II and got cheap housing thanks to the GI Bill. It didn't hurt either that the Los Angeles area also had a thriving business climate.

The house looked and smelled like an old lady's house. Doilies and an old afghan decorated a couch that was so dilapidated that it should have been donated to Goodwill years ago. He walked in, stepping on a threadbare rug covering old, creaky wooden floors.

"Mr. Roark, would you like some tea?"

"No thanks. Just tell me why you waited four months to come forward with information."

"I couldn't, Mr. Roark. Oh, I'm sorry. I should call you by your official name with the police department. You'll have to forgive me. I'm an old lady."

"It's okay. Mr. Roark is just fine. A lot of people call me that."

"Well then, Mr. Roark, as you may know I haven't been at the rectory since...well, since right after Father Tim was murdered. Father Tim. Oh my goodness. I still can't believe it."

"What happened? Father Gregory fire you? I saw the new model for a housekeeper he had. She was quite a dish, if you don't mind me being honest about it."

The old lady smiled, every crease on her face folding into a huge grin, "She should be. She's my daughter."

"What?"

"She was, how do you say it, in the baseball games? Pinch-hitting? Yes. That's it. She was pinch-hitting for me while I was in the hospital. I was having these problems and the doctors said I had to have surgery. So, I..."

"It's okay, Mrs. Wells. It's okay. I just want to know what happened. You said on the phone you saw who might have killed Father Tim. How did you manage that? As I recall you told me you were in the rectory that night and had warmed up dinner for the two priests and left the rectory. so how in the world would you see the possible murderer?"

She smiled again, "After I warmed up dinner, I left the rectory and walked over to the church. It only took me about five minutes. I wasn't moving too quickly then and lord knows I'm not moving too quickly now but it was a short walk."

"Okay. I get it. Why did you go to the church?"

"Well, Mr. Roark. You should know very well what Saturday night means to a Catholic. I went to confession. I knew Father Tim would be there because Father Gregory..."

"Yes, yes. I get that. You went to confession."

"That's why I warmed up the dinner early. Mr. Roark, so I could go to confession. I would never go to Father Gregory. I would be so embarrassed. You know, because he's older. It isn't like I have a lot to confess, a little old lady like me, but it's still embarrassing going to Father Gregory. I don't know why, actually."

"Mrs. Wells, please tell me what you saw."

"I never actually got to confession. I stopped at the door because she was there, in the pew just outside of the confessional. I was just about to enter the church but I hesitated."

"Why, Mrs. Wells?"

"She did the strangest thing. Instead of going in the door where people go to tell the

252

priest their sins she went into the middle door where the priest sits.”

“Are you sure?”

“Just as sure as I'm sitting here. I remember it like it happened just yesterday.”

“So, then what did you do?”

“I just froze. I didn't think regular people were supposed to go in the door where the priest sits.”

“They're not.”

“How long was she in there?”

“I don't know.”

“Could you make a guess. Five seconds? Ten? Longer?”

“I don't know, Mr. Roark, because I wasn't about to stick around and find out what that was all about.”

“Did you hear anything?”

“Well, yes. I heard him make a sound.”

“What sort of a sound?”

“Like he was glad to see her. It was like a yelp. Sort of like a sound a dog makes when his master comes home.”

“A yelp? And that was it?”

“Then I heard her talking to him and so I got out of there in a hurry. It would have been so embarrassing if they had caught me spying on them.”

“Now think, Mrs. Wells. Did you happen to see anybody else in church?”

She shook her head. “No, not that I recall.”

"He would have been walking the stations of the cross."

"I don't think there was anybody there. Besides, it makes no sense."

"Why is that?"

"It's just a strange time to be doing the stations of the cross."

"If you say so, Mrs. Wells. Now, back to my original question. You were in the hospital, for surgery, then whatever. All of sudden you decide to call me. I don't get it."

"Father Gregory told me to call you. That was when I went back to work at the rectory. I relieved my daughter. So, a dish, as you called her, won't be working in the rectory anymore."

"Father Gregory told you to call me?"

"Why, yes. First thing I asked him was whether they found out what happened to poor Father Tim. He told me, as far as he knew, nothing was happening so I told him."

"You told him about the young woman going into the confessional?"

"Well, of course. I thought it would be helpful. I'm sorry I waited so long. You see I was in the hospital and..."

"It's okay, Mrs. Wells. Just tell me. What did she look like?"

"Well, I didn't see her face but she had blonde hair and was improperly dressed, in my opinion."

"Improper? In what way?"

"She was wearing, you know, one of those outfits people wear when they are running. I see them on TV all the time. I suppose they're okay to wear out to some place like the grocery store but I doubt very much they're proper to wear in church."

After Roark left the old ladies house one question began to dominate his thinking. Who was investigating this murder anyway, him or Father Gregory? The old priest seemed to have his hand in everything, directing people to go see him whenever it seemed to divert attention away from himself. Maybe that was it. Father Gregory, the wise-old priest, ex-Marine, was making sure all Roark's attention was directed any place but towards him. The priest who confessed to decking a seminarian. A priest who no doubt bought the guy's silence with a payment of cash, if Culpepper's information was true. All that was cause to wonder.

The old lady's story about Kitty going into the confessional. Interesting, to be sure, but of what evidential value?

CHAPTER FORTY-THREE

Wow. Kitty never told him she entered the confessional through the middle door. That might have had a bearing on the situation. I wonder, thought Roark, why she wouldn't have told me that. And what's with the mystery of the man walking the Stations of the Cross? She says he was there; Mrs. Wells says he was not there. Mrs. Wells is an old lady. She could be mistaken, to be fair about it. How would she know for sure anyway? After all, it's far easier to be sure about a positive thing than it is about a negative thing. If you see a person you can be very definite about. I saw a person. Not seeing a person, there's no way of being sure about that. The only person that would be sure about that would be the person who claimed to see the man in the first place.

He couldn't explain why it continued to bother him so much but it did, the fact that Father Gregory seemed to pop up when least expected to become the pivot man for a new twist in the case. Or, maybe it was just a simple matter of an old lady going to the person she was most comfortable with when she had such important information to share. Still, it bothered him. Just too much of a coincidence or a contrivance.

Back to what he now had to believe as factual. A young blond woman in a running outfit entered the center door of the confessional just before six o'clock, at closing time. Very unusual to say the least. And, to make matters worse, although she couldn't be positively identified by a little old lady who never saw her face, it was clear to Roark who it was. Question now was not if, but why. Why did she do that? Why did she lie about it? Did she kill him or maybe she went in there for another reason? Roark had a horrible thought enter his mind like an uninvited case of the hives. What if she merely went in there to give Father Tim a blow job? That wouldn't have killed him.

Blow job or a knife to the throat, what Mrs. Wells had told him wasn't enough to convict her of anything. He could just hear her lawyer in court cross examining Mrs. Wells on the stand.

"Mrs. Wells, you say you saw a woman enter the middle door of the confessional. Did you see this woman's face?"

"No sir."

"So how do you know it was the defendant, the woman sitting over there?"

"I guess I don't know."

"All right then. Let's just assume for the moment that it was, indeed, the defendant that entered the confessional. Did you see what happened inside that little compartment?"

"No, I did not."

"Thank you, Mrs. Wells. No further questions."

The tale that Mrs. Wells had just told him proved nothing. All it did was upset Roark. He hated lies. Clearly, there was only one solution to this problem. He'd have to torture Kitty Meadows to get her to tell the truth. Torture? How would he go about doing that, he wondered? Then it came to him. I'll force her to eat some frozen food out of the microwave.

It was now time to see where he was, what he had. The old boxing open-handed priest who pays off a possible suspect and manipulates a witness like a person playing chess. Then there's Jablonski, with a new job and sudden wealth. It was convincing enough for Culpepper but then Culpepper's elevator didn't always go to the top floor. As far as he was concerned, Jablonski was still a player. Clever, yes. Very clever. Capable of murder? I think so, thought Roark.

Kitty Meadows? She lies but lying is not a crime. She has a dark side to be sure but then she has a soft, irresistible side. Something else burned in Roark's brain. A woman killing in cold blood? It didn't seem possible no matter how many lies she told. After all, he kept reminding himself, she's the one who came forward and proved to be the only witness who, at that point, was there. No guilty person would have done that. Would they? Roark was unable to answer that question other than to mumble to himself that this case was maddening, enough to drive him nuts before it was over.

CHAPTER FORTY-FOUR

Kitty Meadows was twelve years old when her mother divorced her father and married her new husband. It was a good news, bad news sort of thing. Divorce is never good news for a child of twelve. Well, usually it works that way. There are all the usual questions of why did this happen? Why did my mother and father have sex and give birth to me and then they decide to separate? They decide they hate each other. What does that do to the validity of my existence? She was terribly confused and what made matters worse her mother was always in a bad mood. It was like her mother blamed her for everything, or so she thought.

The new husband, her new stepfather was a nice guy. They moved into his house because he had money, lots of money, more than her mother would ever dream of having. That was good for her mother. Her mother was no longer in a bad mood all the time. What wasn't so special was the fact that she, Kitty, was sort of the odd person out, no longer an integral part of the family. Time and again, when she wanted to talk to her mother; she'd be told to go along and play or do her homework or something, anything, just get out of sight for now. Her mother needed some private time with her new husband.

Her new stepfather was the first to notice that she felt cheated in this new relationship, or the lack thereof. Surprisingly, he came to her rescue, visiting her in her room one night, explaining how he understood, how he knew what she was thinking, how he knew why she was sad. He pledged to her his support to try, as best he could, to gradually turn things around. So, pretty soon, they had nightly conferences to discuss the progress of bringing her back into the fold, so to speak, to make her feel more like a pivotal part of the family again and not just a third wheel who happened to live there and was shuffled off to her room whenever it was inconvenient for her to be in their presence.

The first time seemed innocent enough. He touched her softly and compassionately on her arms and the back of her neck, saying soft, sympathetic words to make her feel better. It was more than her mother had done for her lately, a lot more. In fact, when it came to discipline, her mother seemed to relish chastising her and inflicting punishment more severe than was warranted. Her stepfather, in a private session in her bedroom came to her rescue, soothing her. More touching started to take place.

It didn't take long for the private sessions and the touching to expand its horizons to something more intimate. Her private parts seemed to be the next most logical place for his hands. She became aroused. Somewhere along the line of this series of nightly visits, she wound up doing what he asked her to do.

Where was her mother when all this was going on? At the bottom of a bottle of booze; she saw it but she said nothing. It was now a clear signal for her stepfather to visit her and that was all she needed for the present time.

Clearly, she thought, even as a twelve-year-old, now a thirteen-year-old she had the knowledge to know that what she was doing was not quite right. It felt good and it pleased him and, in a way, that pleased her but she knew in her heart that what they were doing wasn't quite right. She had a choice. Either she could tell him to never again visit her bedroom and lose the one person who seemed to be in her corner, her safety net, the one person who seemed to understand her and her needs or she could try to regain her mother's favor. The choice was easy. A simple sexual act meant nothing to her in any real way. It had no particular meaning other than it was a means to an end. The end was to receive his favor and his approval and that was something she desperately needed. It didn't hurt. It didn't make her feel dirty. In a strange, inexplicable way, it made her feel empowered. She was no longer the victim but, in her mind, the person in charge of the situation.

She just loved it and it gave her a thrill when, as she was servicing him, he'd stroke her hair and the side of face and tell her what a beautiful young lady she was.

Kitty's stepfather teased her with the notion that this was their little secret. Whatever you do, don't tell your mother or she will be extremely jealous and that would cause problems for both of us.

Since there was no harm in what they were doing, why tell her mother anything? Her stepfather had convinced her that, if she told her mother, those kind, beautiful words would stop and, like her stepfather had said, it would cause a lot of problems.

So, the nightly visits continued.

CHAPTER FORTY-FIVE

Roark decided torture might not be the best way to get Kitty Meadows to confess, micro-waved frozen food or no. First of all, confessions resulting from torture were often over-turned in a court of law. So, if she was ever going to confess it had to be something she dearly wanted to do.

Under the guise that he had some interesting news relative to the investigation of the murder he called her and arranged to meet her in the park once again. He decided to fabricate a story to throw her completely off guard. Irregular police work? Sure it was, but what else could he do?

As usual, she looked beautiful. After an embarrassing moment where they both wondered if they should exchange a hug or shake hands, they did neither. He suggested they walk around the lake a bit.

After a while she couldn't contain her curiosity a moment longer. "You said you had some news about Father Tim's murder?"

"Let's sit on the bench for a moment," he said guiding her to a nearby bench that was drenched in sunlight and relatively isolated. She sat halfway facing him and he did the same, purposely, intending to see whatever facial reaction he could see with the statement he was about to make.

"I'm done with investigating the murder of Father Tim. I thought you'd like to know that."

If there was a reaction one way or the other, Roark couldn't read it. After a long couple of seconds and with almost casual indifference she said, "Really, Sebastian. That has to be relief off your mind. So, are you able to tell me who did it?"

"Somebody confessed and they've got him downtown, in a holding pattern, until they can check out his story," he lied with, what he thought was a convincing act.

"Oh, my god, that has to be really good news for you, Sebastian. Does that mean you won't be asking me any more questions?"

"I think that's exactly what it means. No more questions."

"So, this is good-bye? I won't be seeing you anymore?"

He looked away. This was becoming harder than he thought it would be and he suddenly recalled the story of Pinocchio with his nose growing bigger whenever he lied. Then he focused back onto her, looking intently into her eyes. "I was kind of hoping we could go back to where we left off, back at my apartment."

"Sebastian. I'm in shock. If I didn't know any better, I would think you're trying to get me into bed."

"You've got it all wrong, Kitty. What I want is to start over with you and I. I'd like to get to know you better. I'd like for you to get to know me. Do it the right way. You know, instead of the wrong way." Then he grinned. "Not exactly like what we did back at my apartment. Since the investigation is over there's no reason we can't see each other the way people are supposed to see each other."

"Really, Sebastian. You're not just trying to get me to bed, like all the other guys I've known? That would be a first. Not sure I know how to react to that. What exactly did you have in mind?"

"I was thinking just dinner. A nice restaurant. We could talk."

"Like on a date, Sebastian. Is that what you're asking me, to go on a dinner date? Isn't that a little old fashioned?"

"I'm an old-fashioned kind of guy."

Chapter Forty-Six

Kitty honed her skill in pleasing guys. What she learned from her stepfather she perfected with the guys at her high school. Because of those skills she became a very popular girl, maybe the most popular girl in school, hands down, so to speak.

High school was followed by an abbreviated attempt at college. First of all, she found that she didn't like studying. It was just too hard to focus and studying gave her a headache. Whereas she could get by with that sort of attitude in high school, it didn't work well in college. Besides, what purpose would studying serve anyway? What cleared it up for her was one day talking to another girl in one of her classes and they were commiserating about how hard it was to study and what was the purpose of it all and stuff like that and the girl came right out and said it. "Honey, look. Half the girls here are here for one reason and one reason only. To get a husband."

Kitty Meadows took it to heart and that soon became her new goal. Don't worry about studying. Look for a husband.

He was in one of her classes, the guy she targeted first. Once she started to pay attention to him it was time to throw out the net and haul him in. The best way to get him to notice her was to ask him questions about the class. Did he understand something the professor had tried to explain? He was a smart and handsome young man, the perfect combination, in her opinion. He'd make it as a good lover and a potential provider and all the other girls would be so jealous.

It didn't take long for him to ask her out on a date. Within a couple of weeks things got serious and, just when she thought he would make a move on her in a physical way, he surprised her by asking about her belief in God. What a pathetically strange question, she thought to herself...but whatever gets the job done, she was prepared to do it.

Soon she was attending meetings with him at the Newman Club, a Catholic sponsored club at the university. At the meetings she heard all the good things that the Catholic Church had to offer and it didn't hurt a bit that it more or less bound her more closely to her new boy friend. On a weekly basis she began hearing moving presentations and testimonials about the evils of sex and how forming a good Christian marriage was the only way to happiness and eternal salvation. It made some sense to her. It was clearly an awakening of sorts. Being a bad girl wasn't all bad but being a good girl seemed to be the only way to haul in Mr. Right. Too bad it didn't work the way she hoped it would.

It was a nice restaurant. One of those that looked out over the ocean. White linen table cloth, candles lit up, a little flame inside a glass bowl. Very romantic.

So, Roark lifted his wine glass. "A toast. To the end of this case. And, maybe, if you don't object, to *us*."

He asked her mindless, useless questions. Where did she go to high school, what about her family? Her answers got sorted out in the recesses of his brain. He hoped he'd remember some of it but, at the moment, he couldn't care less.

She started to tell him about her fling at UCLA with the religious guy.

Is that when you met Jerry Jablonski?"

"Oh no. That came later. Quite a bit later." She said. She then went on to tell him everything.

"So, what happened? You met the guy; you fell in love. And he wanted you to be a virgin, I suppose." Roark asked, taking another sip of wine.

"I converted." She smiled.

"No, I mean, about the boyfriend."

"Oh, he suddenly got interested in somebody else who was a little more pious and a
little more involved in church. Apparently,
she went to mass every morning and I
thought that was just a little bit too much."

"But you converted anyway?"

"Yeah, I was halfway there, believing all
that stuff. For the first time in my life I had
some purpose, like life had some meaning. I
know it sounds corny but, to a person at
that time in my life that hadn't received any
direction one way or another from anybody,
it served a purpose. And, after all that
happened with my step-father, I needed
something, something to turn my life
around."

He smiled. "You were converting just
about the same time I was going in the opposite direction, whatever the opposite of
converting is. Now, tell me about your step-
father."

"I'd rather not. I think you can guess
what he did to me. Can we talk about
something else? Tell me about you. I'm
tired talking about me. You said something
about going in the opposite direction. What
did you mean?"

"I stopped believing in all that stuff."

"Really? Why?"

He drained his glass and got the attention
of the waitress just in time to avoid her
question and order another round of drinks,
both rich Chardonnays from the wine coun-

try just north of San Francisco. "I'd like to go up there someday," he said.

"Where?"

"The wine country. You know you can spend an entire afternoon just driving from one winery to the next and getting free wine tasting at every winery. So, tell me. What happened to your step-father? Did he ever leave you alone?"

She waited for the waitress to pick up two empty glasses and replace them with two new glasses, each filled about one-third of the way with their second glass of Chardonnay.

"I killed him."

Chapter Forty-Eight

The timing was perfect if you looked at it in a perverted way. He had just taken a generous sip of the new glass of wine when she had announced killing her stepfather. He gasped and uncontrollably spat wine out of his mouth onto the table getting some of it on her."

"You're kidding, right?" He asked after collecting his composure.

"No, I'm serious. I killed him."

Roark shook his head negatively. "If that were true you wouldn't be walking around free and you wouldn't be telling me you did it."

"No, it's true. I killed him."

After the waitress came to their rescue and cleaned up the mess, Kitty went on to explain that the so-called special meetings when he would suddenly visit her bedroom got more intense and when she began to object, he began to threaten her. She then told him she was going to tell her mother and that would make him stop, and it made him quite angry. The sessions did stop for awhile until one night when the two of them, him and her mother, came home drunk and her mother had passed out. Her stepfather saw this as the perfect opportunity to take advantage of his beautiful young stepdaughter who had begun to blossom into young womanhood with delightful breasts at the ripe old age of fourteen. She resisted and he slapped her, slapped her hard. The blow stung her cheek and rattled her brain and pain resonated around in her head, bringing tears into her eyes. He then proceeded to have his way with her and it wasn't at all pleasant, more of a violent act than one of endearment. When he was done, he zipped his pants up and staggered into the living room where he fell asleep on the couch.

"I hurt so bad," she said. "I felt violated. Before, when it was just, well, you know, a little less invasive, it was something that I didn't mind doing. But this time it was different. His breath stunk of alcohol and I could see the wild look in his eyes. It hurt when he came inside me." She paused to decide how much further to go with this tale.

"I think it was his anger and the fact he had slapped me so hard. I couldn't help myself. I started to go find my mother, to see where she was and then I saw him asleep on the couch, totally out. The bastard. All this time, I thought he loved me. He didn't love me; he used me. I couldn't help myself."

Roark was mesmerized just as if he had taken a paralyzing drug. His eyes, glazed over, his ears ringing. He couldn't believe what he was hearing. He looked at her with a big question mark on his face.

She said, "So I got a big knife out of the kitchen and killed him."

Then she went on to explain that her lawyer was successful in convincing a jury that a poor fourteen-year-old child had every right to do what she did having been violated in the worst way, a way that would negatively impact her for the rest of her life. At the trial her mother had shed copious tears explaining how she didn't know what had been happening all those years and how she regretted something like this happening to her beautiful young daughter and, if she only had another chance, she would never let anything like this happen again. It only took the jury two hours to come back with a not guilty verdict.

Roark nodded his understanding, the fact that the non-guilty verdict did not surprise him. What he didn't let on was the fact that an ugly thought was bouncing around in his head.

"I think this is an all too familiar story. I'm sort of surprised you got off, but then I'm not surprised. What bothers me a little is you don't seem to be too remorseful about it."

"Remorse? Not for a minute. He had it coming. I'd do it all over again. Remember, Roark, you weren't there. You've never been a fourteen-year-old girl who's been violated. I've had to live with that for all these years. Remorse? Not for a minute."

"Okay. It's ancient history. I'm not here to judge your past. So, tell me after all that. Then what happened?" He asked.

"I got out of high school, went to UCLA and then met Mr. Right. Then the summer after that I broke up with the guy because he fell in love with Miss Goody-goody," she said it derisively, referring to the other girl. "That's when I met Jerry."

"Don't tell me. You felt rejected and went after the first guy you saw?"

She remained silent, staring out the window of the restaurant. The Pacific Ocean rolled around like a giant mattress, the orange sun setting in the far-off sky.

"He lied to me. Going to UCLA to become a doctor? Wow. Did I ever fall for that, hook, line, and sinker?"

"He got you pregnant."

She laughed, "That was a lie and he fell for it."

Puzzled Roark asked, "You weren't pregnant?"

"Good lord no. You know what's funny. The stupid idiot didn't suspect."

"Suspect what?"

"I told him I was pregnant three weeks after we had sex. What girl knows she's pregnant after three weeks?"

"You got me there. I have no personal experience with that sort of thing. So, you lied about being pregnant and you married the guy?"

"Yeah. The little prick had a conscience. He wanted to do the right thing. Then he promises me he will go to UCLA and become a doctor. I figured okay. Maybe he will. So, we got married."

"What was his reaction when you told him you lied about having a baby?"

"I told him I had a miscarriage. It just flushed down the toilet and he bought it. That was that. I had to pretend of course that I was crushed by the loss. Then I started on the pill so the real thing wouldn't happen."

"That's kind of severe. You didn't want kids?"

"Roark. I've had a tough life. My childhood was not exactly a picnic. I wind up getting married to guy who first wants to be a priest then wants to be a doctor only to find that what he really wants is to come home and get drunk every night. Bring a kid into a situation like that? No way."

Roark asked, "So no kid. He's a drunk and you get divorced?"

"It's as simple as that. Now, how about I ask you a question, Sebastian? You said the case has been solved. You said somebody came by and confessed? I haven't seen anything about that in the news."

Roark was ready to strike, "It's being withheld for a while until we check out some things. Actually, part of the process involves this lady, the one who cooks for the priests. She came by the church just before closing time and she saw the whole thing."

CHAPTER FORTY-NINE

Kitty was the first to respond when the waitress came back to see if they wanted more wine.

"No, we're done," she said. Then to Roark, "I don't need any more wine. Remember what happed the last time." The waitress moved away. "Can we go?"

Roark nodded, "We haven't eaten."

"I'm not hungry. I really want to go. All this talk about my past; it's just really upset me."

Roark made a quick decision. He felt in his heart she was either about to confess her crime just to relieve her conscience and put an end to the torment or she was going to slip up somehow in a way that he'd have some proof that he could take to the court. Either way, he was determined to give her all the leeway she needed and not, in any way, offend her. He was convinced, that once she got offended, she'd clam up and he'd never get to the truth. He consented to leave the restaurant and they drove back to her apartment.

Driving her to her apartment gave him time to think because she was suddenly very reticent. Short of getting her to confess there wasn't much for him to go on. And there was nothing he hated worse than arresting someone, bringing them to justice, in his mind, only to see the accused get off by being found innocent because the evidence failed. Sometimes that was simply the fault of a jury that came in with a totally inexplicable verdict. It does happen, he reminded himself. There are cases where it's simply a road-show where the defending attorney was more theatrical ability and more capable of spinning things around and confusing the jury than were the prosecuting attorneys who, at the end of the day had very little to lose if they lost a case. They still had a job and their defeat was all too soon forgotten. Forgotten that is, if they didn't let it happen too often. Or, sometimes a case is lost because the investigating officers, like him, failed to do their job. That one he hated. He hated all three of the reasons he was presently thinking about, but failing to do his job properly, if he were to do that, would be the bitterest defeat of them all.

Here was the problem with this case in his estimation. Normally, in a murder case, the perpetrator takes the murder weapon and hides it somewhere or, at the very least, the murder weapon is traceable to the perpetrator. Time and again, murder weapons, be it a gun, a knife, or something else, gets dumped into a dumpster or thrown off a bridge. Most of the time, the weapon is found after a laborious effort by law enforcement. Sometimes it takes weeks or months, but the weapon is eventually found. In this case, the weapon stayed with the victim, stuck in his neck.

Something told him she was not going to confess and he couldn't think of a single solitary piece of evidence that she did it. A good lawyer would get her off faster than a fart going through trousers.

"You're awfully quiet," she said suddenly breaking the silence.

"I was thinking. About that housekeeper's testimony."

"What did she say? You said she saw the murderer."

"That is true."

"Well?"

"You know I can't go into that. It's still an on-going investigation."

"But you said you're no longer involved in it."

"True. Other people in the department are taking it from here."

He pulled into the parking lot where her apartment was and shut off the motor, "I do have one question for you."

"You said you're off the case. For somebody who is off the case you're asking a whole lot of questions. I feel like I'm getting the third degree."

He laughed, "I'm just curious. That's my nature."

"You know what happened to the cat that got too curious."

He laughed again, "You went to the church to go to confession?"

"No. I didn't. I told you. I went there to talk to Father Tim. I knew that's the one place he couldn't escape from me. Do you really think I'd confess my sins to the man I loved?"

"You seem to love all the wrong people."

"That's a horrible thing to say."

"Sorry. I didn't mean it to come out that way. You know what I meant."

"No, I don't"

"I just meant; how could you fall in love with a priest when you knew he was married to the Church?"

"Call me foolish. I thought he loved me and was ready to leave the priesthood. We talked about it."

"And?"

"At one point he said he would."

"You got your hopes up."

She paused to think, "Yes, I really did. No question he was a giant step up from Jerry and all the others. He was kind and he treated me like I'd never been treated before." She looked at Roark to judge his reaction. In the dim light of the car after the sun had set it was hard to judge it.

She continued, "You don't believe me. You have no idea how important that was to me."

He shrugged his shoulders. Now she was encouraged to go further.

"We made plans. We talked about jobs he would get and where we might live." Roark nodded. "I suppose you think we were evil. We really weren't."

"He was a priest."

"It's no sin to leave the priesthood. That's what he told me. Then, a few weeks later he told me he just couldn't do it. He told me we just couldn't see each other anymore. He wished me luck. He even said he was sure I'd find somebody more deserving. But he's the man I wanted. He just didn't understand that."

"Okay, you went to the church to talk to him because that was the only way you'd have him as a captured audience. And?"

"I begged him."

Roark was so close. He knew though he had to be careful. He changed course, "You came to me, that first week. Why?"

"Why? I thought you'd want to know there was a man there."

"The other witness, the old lady who cooks, she said there was no man there."

"Oh my God," she said putting her hand up to her face, almost smashing her nose. "I can't believe this."

"What?"

"You believe the other witness; an old lady who knows God knows what, over me. I think I know what that means. If there was no other man in the church then that only leaves me and Father Tim and that means, oh my god, Sebastian, you think, you think it was me who did it."

Chapter Fifty

"I hate you," she screamed as she ran out of the passenger side of the car, slamming the door. "I hate you."

Roark was stunned for a moment. He was certain she was going to run up the stairs to her apartment and there was no point in running after her. He had no right to invade her apartment if she refused to let him in. Instead, he saw her running away from the apartment building, down the street. Instinctively, he got out of the car and ran after her. There was no private space now in which to hide so he decided he'd do it; he'd chase her down.

What he found out in a hurry was a woman who runs a lot and wearing a dress and flats can run a bit faster than a guy wearing dress pants and loafers and who hadn't run anywhere in years. He not only was not catching up to her; he was losing ground. After a couple of blocks, he began to question the wisdom of chasing after her. What was the point?

Then he realized where she was headed. MacArthur Park was just ahead if he was not mistaken, some three or four more blocks. Why would she go there of all places? It made no sense but he kept running, ever more slowly as he began to tire, his lungs cramping, his legs burning. *Okay, enough of this crap,* thought Roark. *I'm stopping.*

The lake. Oh my god, he thought. *She's running to the lake in the middle of the park. She wouldn't, would she?* He picked up the pace again. If she did, and was determined to kill herself, murderer or no murderer, he would feel he was to blame. He had to go after her. He only hoped he'd get there in time.

Suddenly the park was just across the street. No cars were coming and he forced himself to keep going although his lungs were bursting. It seemed like his throat was constricted, as he gasped for air. His hips hurt; his knees hurt.

He reached the park, just before collapsing. Bent over with his hands on his knees, he looked left, then right, but didn't see her in either direction. All this for naught; she's in the lake and there's nothing he could do about it. Not only was he a poor athlete but swimming was never high on his list of activities. Sure, he could swim all right but not enough to save himself and a woman determined to drown herself.

He sat on a convenient bench, panting, continuing to gasp for breath. Pain welled up in his upper chest and throat. He could feel his temples were throbbing like they were laced with electric wires all firing in sporadic sparks. He was going to die; he was certain of it.

What a way to die, he thought, in a futile effort to catch a foolish woman who was a murderer. All sorts of things raced through his head. With him being gone would his replacement nail down Kitty Meadows as the murderer, if she were still alive? If dead, would she ever be found to be the murderer postmortem? Then he decided he really shouldn't care one way or the other. If he died right there on the spot, on that bench, why should he care what happens to Kitty Meadows?

A hand gently touched his shoulder. "Are you all right?" A female voice asked. With his temples pounding it seemed to affect his hearing. He looked up.

Kitty was standing there, her hand still resting on his shoulder. He could barely speak. It came out sounding like a cough, "I thought you were gone?"

"Gone? Where would I go?"

He swallowed hard and cleared his throat, "I thought you (cough) jumped in the lake."

"This is a hell of time to be taking a swim," she said laughing.

"I agree but then why the (cough) hell did you run over here?"

"This is where I run every day. This is where I do it. It's as natural for me as brushing my teeth. Where else would I go?"

He was starting to feel better and was willing to bet there was an even chance he was going to live, "I thought maybe you were going to kill yourself, in the lake."

She turned to look at the lake that was now barely visible in the dark, "That lake? If I was going to kill myself, I don't think I'd pick that lake?"

"Why not?"

"I heard it's man-made. I doubt it's more than four feet deep."

She really didn't know one way or the other, it just sounded good, like something to say to put his mind at ease.

They walked back to her apartment and a lot slower on the return trip. He was breathing normally now and was beginning to feel a lot better.

"Are you going to make it?" She asked noticing that he was walking very gingerly. "Do you need my help?"

"I'm fine. I just got blisters on my feet. Not used to running in these shoes."

Chapter Fifty-One

In her apartment, she washed and bandaged his feet. Both had ugly blisters, white patches about the size of a quarter on the balls of both feet. The worst part was the iodine she patted onto the sore spots.

"Ouch, that hurts," He exclaimed.

"Baby, I thought you were a tough guy?"

He ignored her.

"Did you really think I was going to kill myself? Why?"

"Oh, I don't know. Maybe a guilty conscience; people have been known to do that."

"Guilty conscience; you still think I harmed Father Tim?"

"The woman saw you. The housekeeper who cooks for the priests, whatever she was. She said she saw you go into the confessional where the priest sits."

She finished with his feet and put his socks back on again.

"There. I think you're good now. There won't be any charge for taking care of you."

She got up and went to the kitchen sink and washed her hands, drying them thoroughly on a cloth kitchen towel.

"Yes, Sebastian. I did enter the section where the priest sits. I wanted to see him face to face and not through a small screen where he looked like he was a phantom or a ghost. I wanted one last time to see his eyes. I wanted him to see me for the last time like a real person. He didn't like it, when I did it."

"You did it then?"

"Yes. I kissed him on the cheek and told him I wouldn't bother him ever again."

"Are you sure about that?"

She hesitated, "You know you were right what you said when we were sitting in the car."

"I was right?" Roark asked wondering if this was the moment he'd been waiting for.

"Yes. You said I just keep falling in love with the wrong people. I go from a loser like Jerry Jablonski, to a priest that, as it turned out, I could never have. Am I sure about the fact I kissed him on the cheek? Absolutely."

Chapter Fifty-Two

Roark laid down on his bed ready for sleep. It had been a long day. The blisters on his feet were still stinging a bit but, other than that, he seemed to be fully recovered from a very scary attempt at running longer and faster than he should have done. He learned his lesson. If man were meant to run, he reasoned, he would have four feet.

The phone rang just as he put his head on the pillow. He put it to his ear. Whoever was calling him this time of the night either knew him or was an obscene phone call. "Yeah?"

"Roark?" a familiar man's voice asked.

"Yeah."

"It's me, Roy. Did you hear the news?"

"I've been busy, Roy boy, what do you want?"

"They think they've found the guy who did in that priest. You know the case you and I were working on."

Roark sat up in bed and switched the phone to his left ear, the side where he usually listened to important phone calls.

"What are you talking about?"

"Another murder. Some guy tried to kill another priest in the same way as the case you were working on. Only difference was he got caught. Turns out there was a second priest in the other confessional. He heard the noise just in time to come out and confront the perp. He got cut up a little but he and the first priest, between the two of them, they got the guy down and called the police."

"Culpepper, this better not be one of your sick jokes."

"Honest, on my mother's grave, Roark. Would I shit you about something like this? The guy confessed."

CHAPTER FIFTY-THREE

Now that it was all over and Roark had taken a couple of days off, he had a thought. He felt it honorable, if not absolutely necessary, that he visit Father Gregory. The case was over. Yet, there were things he wanted to say, things to clear the air. Maybe make an apology along the way. Roark only hoped the old priest hadn't yet moved on to another parish or retired. Fortunately, he found him still at the rectory. He hadn't moved yet.

When he arrived the old priest's library of books was empty as was his desk. A mere shadow of his former presence.

"I suppose you're getting tired of me by now, Father?"

"Not in the least, Inspector. As I said, I always enjoyed your visits. Well, that is, until you started accusing me of things."

"Forgive me, Father. It's my job to be obnoxious. Somebody's got to do it."

"I suppose. As you can see, I'm almost completely packed up. The new pastor got delayed a week so here I am, still on duty." The priest looked up toward the heavens, deep in thought or maybe he was praying.

"So, the man confessed, the man you mentioned on the phone? He confessed to killing Father Tim? But why?"

"That's just it, Father. From what I hear, he had no connection whatsoever to Father Tim. There was no reason other than, and I hate to say this but, he mentioned he had been a victim of priest abuse. I didn't talk to him but that's what I'm told he said. He had been victimized and he had tried to get the Church to admit that and pay him money. Apparently, it never happened so he decided to seek revenge in the only way he knew how."

Father Gregory shook his head solemnly. "Sad. Really sad. There's no denying, I guess, there have been instances of that sort of thing. But it's so rare that it happens. It's like one bad apple spoiling the entire barrel."

Roark tried to be agreeable, if not sympathetic, but it didn't come out that way. "One time is maybe one time too many, Father. Plus I'm thinking there's a lot more than just one bad apple."

"You can be very judgmental, Inspector."

"It goes with the territory."

The priest nodded his assent, "Yes, I suppose it does," Then he paused. "It's ironic, is it not, that the man, whoever he was, just happened to take it out on a really good priest?"

"Not to speak ill of the dead but I hear he had his problems."

The priest nodded, knowingly, "Priests are men, Inspector. We have our temptations just like anybody else. The difference is we, generally, control those urges. Yes, Father Tim, fell from grace. He was a man. But he didn't violate young boys. He fell to the wiles of a beautiful woman. He repented. He's entitled to forgiveness. That's what the Church is all about, Inspector. Christ died on the cross to make amends for all our sins. All we have to do is repent and confess."

"I'll leave you now, Father. I hope, in the end, you'll not judge me too harshly. It's nothing personal but I hope we don't meet again, at least not under these circumstances. But I do have one parting question. I saw your picture in the yearbook. You were there, in Camarillo. An educator or admin or something."

"Yes, about five years I was there. What of it."

"You're telling me, that during all that time there wasn't a certain amount of hanky-panky going on with all those young men in close quarters, eating, sleeping, playing together; they never played a little too intimately?"

"All right, Inspector. One last question; one last answer. Pedophilia occurs, in my opinion, when a priest is alone and lonely and involved in a one of one situation with a young boy. I'm not saying it's normal, I'm just saying that's when it occurs. In Camarillo, or any seminary, for that matter, yes, there are a lot of young men, as you say, eating, sleeping, playing together. That's the key. There is just too much activity going on as a group. There's no privacy to speak of. If something were to happen it would circulate like a brush fire. And let me give you a clear example of how strict it is there. When any seminarian goes to change his pants and get ready for sleep you would think he'd just drop his drawers and put on his pajamas or whatever he was going to sleep in. No, that's not the way it happens, Roark. The seminarians are taught to put their bathrobe on and then, protected by the bathrobe, they drop their drawers. That's how strict it is. So, Inspector, I'd say no. There's no hanky-panky going."

Roark nodded that he understood not necessarily that he agreed.

"I guess that's it then," he added.

"Well, Inspector, before you go. If you don't mind, I have a question for you?" Roark was half out of his chair but then, politely, settled back down. "What drove you away?"

Roark was taken aback by that question. He stiffened, "I suppose I could point to a lot of little things like too many stupid rules. No meat on Friday. Have to go to mass every Sunday. I guess I don't like rules. But I think the real reason is I just stopped believing."

The priest looked sad, his eyes telling the complete story, a story that he'd faced many times. "You've lost faith in something very important, Inspector. The most important thing that there is in life; how we got here. Why we're here and where do we go after we die. You don't believe the truths that are there because you don't see any tangible evidence. But it's all there in the Bible. It's all there, Inspector. You just have to open your heart and mind."

Roark remained silent.

"Look at it this way," the priest said seeing Roark was raising no defense. "An ant doesn't know a thing about electricity, doesn't have a clue why it is or what it is. Yet, it's there. I liken us mortals to be like ants. We have limited powers, limited amounts of knowledge but, clearly, there are things out there that we don't understand. But they're out there."

Roark got up to leave, "You're probably right, Father, but we're not ants and we're not talking about electricity."

Chapter Fifty-Four

Sea gulls flew in haphazard patterns, barely missing colliding into each other, squawking and squawking in their never-ending search for prey. Occasionally one of them would dive to the ocean surface to be rewarded with a morsel, some not so rewarded either fight with the lucky gull or just give up, only to return to the sky and continue to fly about in a haphazard manner. The ocean rolled in and onto the beach at Santa Monica. Joggers jogged; kids played in the sand building sand castles that have a shelf life of only a few hours until high tide. Brave swimmers hopped up and down in the waves. Nothing seemed to change from one day to the next. It was early September and the beach season was almost over, totally over for some but, for others, they hung onto the last few days.

Roark convinced her that a walk on the beach would be a welcome change and certainly innocent enough. He said to Kitty, as they walked along the sand in the late afternoon sun, she in her usual running outfit, he in slacks and tennis shoes, "What will you do now?"

"I think it's time for me to leave town. By the way, remember the other night, when we went to the restaurant. I really appreciate what you were saying. That maybe we could start over. I was really flattered. Really, I was. But you know what? I just don't think it would work, you and I. I'm sorry, Roark. You're a nice guy but I just don't..."

He cut her off, "It's okay. No need to explain. I think you're probably right. I'm probably not the right guy for you. I'm not sure I'm the right guy for...*well*...never mind. It doesn't matter. So, you're leaving town? San Diego?"

"Yeah. How 'bout you? You staying here in this crazy town?"

Roark took some time to answer, "Except for the Navy, Los Angeles is all I've ever known."

That seemed to be the end of that discussion, no further words needed to be said.

"Think I'll try San Diego. I hear it's nice down there, not so crowded," she said breaking the silence.

Roark thought about that. She was moving out of town and his instant reaction was that's a good thing. He wouldn't have to think about her anymore. He wouldn't be tempted to try to get something started between the two them. Been there, done that, thought Roark to himself.

"I do have one last question," he said.

"Roark, when do you ever stop asking questions?"

Once again, Roark was reminded of the fact she stopped calling him Sebastian, now switching to Roark. The former was endearing the way she said it. The latter was like calling someone you'd happen to meet in a shopping mall.

"It goes with the territory. Anyway, hear me out. You say you saw this guy in the church. The housekeeper says there was no one else in the church. I think this is where we left off a couple of nights ago when you ran out of the car. Anyway, I'm just wondering. Could you have been mistaken? Is it possible you saw something else? A shadow caused by a flickering light? It just bothers me that two witnesses are saying opposite things."

"She's an old lady and I saw what I saw. He was on the opposite side of the church. If she came in the back door, that's in the center of the church, the church was dark. She probably just looked down the center aisle and didn't see anybody. He was on the far side of the church, hidden behind a number of pillars. One minute I'd see him and the next minute he'd be behind a pillar. No wonder she didn't see him."

"Okay," Roark said turning towards her with his hands out, palms facing upward. "I get it. Thanks for clearing that up for me."

"You'll never change, will you? You still don't believe me."

"You're wrong about that, Kitty. I have changed and I have you to thank for that. You see, without there being this mystery guy, the guy who confessed just might be making it up. But, if you're right, and I now fully believe you, then his story has legs. So, I have to thank you for that. You've cleared that up for me because it was bothering me."

"I think it's time to give it up, Roark. I think you need to go on to something else."

"I suppose you're right. Maybe I should be careful of what I wish for. Another crime will come along. Maybe tomorrow; who knows?"

There followed a silence as they kept walking aimlessly. Finally, he said, "I have something else to thank you for. Well, you and some female doctor."

"What?"

"Over the past three to four months I've been working out regularly in the gym and I feel much better. I feel it in my arms and shoulders. More strength. I have more energy. And it feels good."

"You didn't look you had much energy the other night when you tried to catch me."

"I guess weight-lifting and running are two different things. I'll have to go to work on that."

"What does that have to do with me?"

"The night you came over to my apartment."

"You remember that?"

"Not for the reason you're thinking. I remember you put me to shame for eating poorly and I took it to heart."

"Mr. Tough Guy. So, you learned how to cook? You're a man of many talents."

"Not exactly, I got it covered though."

"Then you don't need me."

He didn't answer.

They walked a bit more then she got maudlin.

"Did you really think I was going to throw myself in the lake and you ran like a goat to save me? How sweet. I'm deeply moved. I didn't know you had it in you."

He waved it off.

"You know," he said changing the subject. "This is the second time, recently, I've walked on this beach."

"You got another girl, Sebastian? Somebody you've been holding out on me? I'm jealous," She laughed to make sure he understood.

"It was your ex-husband."

"Jerry? You walked on the beach with Jerry? I didn't know he was your type."

"I had questions. It just happened we were walking towards the beach. He told me a lot of things."

"About he and I, when we were married?"

"Yes. A lot."

She started to ask the normal question of what and why and things like that but decided to ignore the situation.

"It's time, Roark. I'd like to get to San Diego before it gets too late."

"You have a place to stay?"

"I've got it covered."

"You have some money?"

"Like I said, I've got it covered. I'd kiss you good-bye but something tells me that's not the right thing to do."

"I'll walk you to your car."

Turning away from the ocean they made their way over coarse, still warm sand and onto a paved walkway along which they could walk to find her car. Neither one of them said anything. When they found it, he could readily tell a lot of things were stuffed in the back seat. "Looks like you're ready and packed."

"Yep. I'm hitting the road, Sebastian. It's been nice knowing you. Sorry we had to meet under these circumstances."

There was an embarrassing moment as neither of them, separated by just a couple of feet, knew quite what to do next. She unlocked her door and Roark opened it for her, allowing her to quickly get into the driver's seat.

"I better go," she said. "I need gas. Almost on empty."

"Yeah, you wouldn't get very far that way."

CHAPTER FIFTY-FIVE

Knowing that she had to stop for gas gave him just enough time to get to his car and hopefully catch up to her. No particular reason stuck in his mind; just a cop's intuition. Part of him wondered if she was simply going somewhere else in the city or truly going south. Not that it mattered. Well, it did matter. If she was simply moving to someplace else in the city why would she lie about it? Just curious. That was his nature. That probably means she's found somebody, a guy, who's more than happy to take her to his cave.

Driving towards the interstate freeway he looked at every gas station to see if she was parked at a pump. There were so many gas stations in Los Angeles, probably more gas stations than any place in the world. So far, no sign of her car and he was halfway to the interstate, which was, he estimated about five to ten miles from the beach. There soon wouldn't be enough time and he'd run out of time and gas stations.

This whole thing about a guy confessing to the murder of Father Tim still bothered him. Too often people confess to crimes they did not commit. Why? Notoriety. Some form crazed idealism? Sometimes, he hated to admit it, but the police would force it out of whoever they might have in custody. In any event, getting back to this particular case, why would the guy have confessed to a murder that occurred four months earlier? *Why?*

I guess, thought Roark, *because you don't get punished any more for two murders than one murder.* But wait. Something's wrong here. Roark knew it.

The crime of attempted murder like the one he committed and was caught red-handed didn't call for the gas chamber. Why confess to one that did?

Usually, when a person confesses to a crime the police will insist that he or she provide details of the crime, details that no one other than the murderer would know about. When Roark first got the news from Culpepper, that phone call late in the evening, he asked Culpepper about that. Culpepper didn't know. Surprise, surprise. So, the next day he asked the Commissioner about that. Had the guy provided those crucial details or was he, knowing he was a dead man in any event, just blowing off some hatred for the Church?

He was told by the Commissioner to leave it alone. That sounded fishy to him. Reasons for that? There had to be reasons for that, he imagined.

"Why stir up trouble? Let's put this to bed, Roark," she had explained. "You've worked on it for four months and have gotten nowhere. Leave it alone. The last thing we want is to open up old wounds."

Old wounds? Whose old wounds would be opened up? There were no answers forthcoming. So, over the last few days it had continued to plague him, keeping him awake at night. There was just something a little untidy about this. It was too convenient. It struck him as quite easy for a guy to tell enough about the crime to pass as telling the truth. Just about all details of the crime were in the newspaper, the place, the name of the victim, how he died, the weapon etc. Anyone could have confessed to that crime and provided enough details to convince a police department that was more than happy to close the case.

Thinking so hard, he drove right past her car. Two blocks before the interstate she had finally pulled in to a gas station. He quickly pulled over to the side of the busy street and waited for her to pass him by. He waited.

When she pulled out, she then passed him not more than ten feet away from the exact spot he was sitting, totally unaware of his presence.

CHAPTER FIFTY-SIX

When Roark got back to his apartment, he pulled out a stiff drink, straight vodka, and drank half a glass, swallowing the burning liquid. The burn was sharp. When it subsided, he was more careful with the last half of the glass, switching to sipping mode rather than gulping. With his new diet, he'd given up beer and wine. Too many calories, he was told. So, he switched to the hard stuff. It was quicker and more effective. It got him where he wanted to be without having to wait. He poured another glass of vodka, this time adding some ice and he retreated to his couch.

Arriving at the freeway entrance ramp, he had expected her to head south, towards San Diego. Instead, much to his surprise, she took the second turnoff and headed north, towards the Valley. Maybe Santa Barbara. Maybe San Francisco.

He looked at the half empty glass of vodka, a couple of cubes of ice, floating in the liquid. He rattled the ice to make them go chink, chink. Then he downed what was left of the vodka, the ice hitting him in the nose.

She probably did it, he concluded. And she didn't want him following her to San Diego. Going north, there were some five hundred miles of places she could hide. Only 150 miles, going south, before getting to the Mexican border.

Now that the case was closed, life got back to normal for Roark and he couldn't have been happier. This case was just simply too much, for any number of reasons. He hoped he'd never have another one like that one ever again. Talking to Culpepper, of all things, even had its bright side.

"What are you going to do now, Roark, now that your case is solved?"

Roark shrugged his shoulders. He didn't care.

"Well, you can't win 'em all. Anyway, it was a pleasure working with you, Roark. I learned a lot. Too bad we won't be working together anymore."

"Huh?"

"I got transferred downtown. I guess they needed my particular expertise down there."

Without much fanfare, Culpepper quickly packed his gear and they parted company with an awkward handshake. Roark wished him well and thanked him for his help, even though he didn't mean it.

He drove home promising himself he'd take a day off. He hadn't done that since the case had started. Even on Sundays he was doing something if nothing else than sorting the cards on his card table or playing out, in his mind, how each suspect could have done it. Now there was nothing to think about. Maybe he'd just go to a baseball game. The Dodgers were at home and they were in the race for the pennant.

Next day, he woke up wondering. The guy who did it. Too bad he never got a chance to talk to him. *I wonder,* thought Roark, *whether he'll get the death penalty or not. Probably not.* Charles Manson was still alive and look at what he did, brutally killing a pregnant actress and all those other people for absolutely no discernible reason what-soever and he was still alive.

The death penalty in California. It had a well-chronicled and dramatic history to be sure. Too many people had sat on death row for years while their appeals wound around in a lower court and then a higher court. Some got off; some didn't. Those that were scheduled to die were often granted a deferment by whatever Governor happened to live in Sacramento, just minutes before the fatal hour.

The most famous of them all was the case of Caryl Chessman, a convicted kidnapper, rapist and murderer. How many years did he sit on death row? How many years did he and his lawyers appeal? How many times did he come close to dying? His story was so famous somebody wrote a book about it and, maybe even a movie, too. He couldn't remember. What he did remember was Chessman got what he deserved in the end - execution. But it didn't come easy. The Supreme Court of California actually granted a stay of execution one more time, seconds before the end. The order just never got to prison, is what he had heard.

CHAPTER FIFTY-SEVEN

He couldn't help himself. It was just too troublesome a thought that he couldn't get it out of his head. Until he looked into this, he knew he'd never have peace of mind ever again.

She welcomed him with little, if any, warm enthusiasm into her office, a grungy little space considering she was a lawyer. Case law books everywhere, notes, papers. Her desk was a mess.

"This is highly unusual, Detective Roark. I thought you were working the other side."

"I think I'm working the side of justice. At least that's what I thought I was anyway."

She advised him, in no uncertain terms, that her job was to defend the man who would be standing trial for the attempted murder of a priest for which he was caught red-handed and for the confessed murder of Father Tim Hanrahan and there was no way she was going to jeopardize her defense.

He asked her how she came to grips with defending a confessed murderer. Her only statement was "He has a right to the best defense I can give him. It's my job."

Roark was tempted to pursue it further, to ask what she really thought, but thought better of it. He didn't need to hear anymore platitudes about American justice and innocent until proven guilty and all that stuff. He'd spent too many years on the other side, as she had labeled him. He had another purpose in talking to her.

"Do you believe his confession?"

She looked annoyed, "That's not a question I want to answer. Plus, it has no relevance."

"Maybe not to you but to me it has a lot of relevance."

"What are you after, Detective? Whatever it is, I can't help you. I have a client to defend. And, quite frankly, I find this entire meeting to be just a bit unprofessional. I shouldn't even be talking to you."

EPILOGUE

On the plane to San Francisco he had it all sorted out in his mind, exactly, what he needed to do and what he needed to say.

Most reluctantly, and with a frown on her face, Kitty ushered him into her apartment.

"How did you find me?"

"We have our methods."

"I'm guessing," she said as she retreated to the kitchen. "This is not a social call."

"No, Kitty, it's not. I'm placing you under arrest for the murder of Father Timothy Hanrahan. You have the right to remain silent; anything you say can be taken down and used against you in a court of law. You have the right to an attorney."

Roark brought along a female uniformed cop to help with the arrest and as the three of them waited in the terminal for the flight back to Los Angeles, she excused herself.

"I'll be right back. You two don't go anywhere, okay?"

"Hmmm," commented Roark dryly, after she left. "A female cop with a sense of humor and a nervous bladder. What could be next?"

315

Kitty turned to him with sad eyes, "What did it? What did I miss?"

"You were right all along, Kitty. The mystery guy was there, just like you said."

"So, it's him or me. One of us had to do it. <u>Why did it have to be me</u>?"

"He described you perfectly, running suit, blonde hair and all. That makes two viable witnesses."

Her lips began to tremble slightly. He wasn't sure if she was going to cry or scream and create a scene in the airport.

"You don't know what it's like Roark, to be a woman who's been used and abused all her life by just about every man she's ever met. All I've ever been was a sex object. You're a man so what would you know about it."

"And Father Tim?"

"He was my last hope. He was the only man I'd ever met who treated me nice."

"For that he had to die? Remind me to never treat you nice."

She winced, "He promised me. Just like all the others, he promised me. I just couldn't bear it one more time and to be disappointed like that by a priest, a man I admired - and loved. I..."

"Don't say any more. I don't want to hear any more. Just answer me one question. Why on earth did you come forward that day in the police station? Why put yourself right there, as a person of interest?"

"I knew sooner or later you'd find out I was there and then you'd be suspicious," her face then turned from sad to a look of hatred, a look Roark had not seen before. "I figured if I came forward, you'd never suspect me and I could control you rather than the other way around. It seemed to work. I got you to go to bed with me. I fixed your goddamned tender feet that night you got blisters. It was something I wanted to do for a long time. Be in control of a man instead of the other way around."

For Roark it was time for a final assessment. He was convinced she did it. The guy who previously had confessed to doing it? His lawyer, the lady who basically kicked Roark out of her office, called him.

"He's ready to talk," she said. "I guess he's not ready to die for a crime he didn't commit. I don't suppose I should be telling you this but he says the priest was already dead."

"Already dead?"

"Yes, Detective. As in recently deceased."

"Yeah, but that's just his word against hers."

Roark thought about the jury trial that was yet to come. The mystery man now converted to a witness will be cross examined by Kitty's lawyer. He imagined it in his mind.

"You, sir. You claim that you intended to kill the priest but when you went into the confessional to do it, the priest was already dead, a knife sticking in his throat? You say this was right after you saw her go into the confessional? How do we know you're not lying and you actually killed the priest yourself? We have it on record you confessed to this murder. Now you've changed your story. How do we know you're not lying? Did you receive in exchange for this testimony a lesser crime being charged to you? Did you make a deal with the district attorney?"

Somehow or another, Roark imagined, the attorneys would put a twisted spin on the testimony. The jury would, more than likely, not know who to believe.

As they were landing in Los Angeles Roark smiled. He was the only one who really knew the answer to that question.

Kitty broke the silence. She told him everything was a pack of lies. "You believed just about everything I ever told you," she said back in San Francisco. "You need to learn how to not be so gullible, Roark."

"You're the one that's under arrest, my dear," Roark said sarcastically.

She pouted briefly then looked to see if the policewoman could overhear what she was about to say over the roar of the plane's engine. Fortunately, the policewoman sitting across the aisle was deeply immersed in a magazine and not paying any attention to Kitty or Roark. Kitty's expression turned to one of satisfaction, totally contrary to her apparent present predicament.

"You know, Roark, you can't prove a thing. I'll deny everything," she whispered.

Roark pondered that comment, looking a bit worried, then he smiled.

"Not a problem, Kitty. Remember when you were telling me about your boyfriend at UCLA, the one you fell in love with and then dumped you?"

"Yeah, what about it?"

"I found the guy. You were so bent on telling me everything. You even told me the guy's name."

"So what? What does he have to do with this?"

"I paid him a visit. He lives here in town. Wasn't hard to find him."

"Good for you. So, you're good at finding people. So what?"

Roark's smile turned from subtle to priceless, "He identified the knife."

Kitty's eyes glazed over like she'd been shot with a taser, leaving her powerless.

Seeing she couldn't speak, Roark spoke for her.

"Remember you told me he cared so much about you, when you two were in love, that he gave you a knife he got from his father who had died in the War? Since you insisted on jogging around the campus at night, he wanted you to have protection. And, as you said, it was the only thing you got out of the relationship. You kept the knife. You spoke of it as if it were a trophy."

"You bastard."

Roark thought for a moment. It was more or less a mental victory lap.

"We'll just have to let the jury decide your fate, won't we?"